REGRESSION

Tony Cane-Honeysett

AUTHOR'S NOTE

When I was in my early thirties and living in Los Angeles, I was regressed by someone who was relatively new to this form of hypnotism. It was a very strange but fascinating experience for me, and one that I can still recall with vivid clarity. The actual process seemed to take five or six minutes though I was told afterwards that an hour had passed. My mind took me back to an Austrian village around 1750 and the person I saw in my purported previous incarnation was a very overbearing and unpleasant person, even though I understood him to be me. Apparently, I was taken back to the moment of my death which seemed to greatly concern my Regressor who was relieved when I came back to full consciousness, seemingly none the worse. And that begs the question.....what if I hadn't?

CHAPTER ONE

The artsy wine and cheese party was in full swing at Lucy Carvallo's stylish downtown Chicago loft home. The bubbly host was entertaining an eclectic assortment of guests in celebration of her new business venture and the forty or so guests were chatting, drinking and mingling. At thirty-five, there was something about Lucy that gave her a certain je ne sais quoi. She had a European flare about her that maybe her raven, ringlet hair emphasized, courtesy of the genes she'd inherited from her Italian grandfather.

The doorbell rang and Lucy went to greet her latest arrivals. "Mary Jane Jeffries! So great to see you...both." Lucy's beaming smile weakened when she saw the scruffy, pasty-faced husband of her old friend was standing with her. Nevertheless, she greeted them warmly and led the two new arrivals into the slightly less crowded kitchen.

"Brought you this," said Mary Jane, handing the party host a bottle of rather cheap Chardonnay. Lucy accepted it graciously. "Thank you, MJ."

"You remember Tim?" Mary Jane smiled.

"Of course. Hello, Tim."

"Hi," Tim gruffed, sounding like he'd rather be home watching paint dry.

"Been a while, MJ. Must be about five months since I've seen you. Where have you been?"

"I know," shrugged Mary Jane. "Well, you know how it is."

"What can I get you both to drink? We have red, white, Cabernet, Chardonnay...."

"Oh, whatever's open is fine," said Mary Jane rather awkwardly and a little out of her element in the rather swish, contemporary downtown setting.

"Tim? How about you?"

"Got any beer?" he muttered, scratching his three-day old stubble. Lucy opened the fridge and handed him a chilled bottle of Stella Artois.

"There you go, Tim." Lucy put Mary Jane's bottle of wine in the fridge and poured her a glass of a rather pricey but delicious Rombauer Chardonnay. "Come into the living room and meet some guests." Lucy led them both into a large open reception room, filled with exquisite furnishings and large abstract paintings on the expansive white walls.

Across the room studying one particularly intriguing artwork, was Derek Landers; handsome, muscular and dressed immaculately in a sharp black suit and white silk shirt with one button too many undone. As he admired the Pollack-esque piece with a slight tilt of his head whilst cupping his glass of Cabernet in his palm, he looked like a male model out of Harper's. Derek glanced over to see Mary Jane approaching. A smile crept over his face though he was somewhat surprised to see her husband traipsing behind in scruffy jeans and old sneakers.

"Hello, Derek," Mary Jane beamed.

"You guys know each other?" Lucy frowned, curiously.

"We're neighbors," Derek and Mary Jane said simultaneously, both laughing at their synchronicity.

"So how do you two hot chicks know each other?" Derek smirked, looking at Lucy and Mary Jane. Both women pulled faces.

"Oh, we go back a way. Mary Jane introduced me to my ex."

"And we're still friends!" Mary Jane laughed. Tim took a swig of his Stella and ignored the conversation.

"Hello, Tim," said Derek, without offering to shake his hand. Tim swigged his beer again rather than acknowledge Derek was even in the room, setting off internal alarm bells for both women although Lucy wasn't going to let it dampen the cool vibe of her party.

"Derek and I met at my new art gallery," Lucy enthused. "He was looking for a painting of Tuscany for someone special, so I introduced him to Cannevechio and Grimaldi. Figuratively, of course, not literally! They've both been dead for a hundred years." Mary Jane hadn't heard of either artist and showed little interest in knowing more while her husband seemed more engrossed with staring at everybody's shoes. Lucy picked up on Tim's socially awkward behavior. "Anyway…that's how we became friends," Lucy finished abruptly.

"Hmmm…Is that right?" Mary Jane smiled, looking directly at Derek with a teasingly suspicious tongue-in-cheek expression.

"Yep, true story," Derek winked back.

"Derek paints a little too, apparently," Lucy added.

"That's true, too," he nodded.

"What a talented man you are, Derek," Mary Jane smirked.

"Well, I don't really call myself an artist per se," Derek continued, "I just fool around a bit." Tim belched loudly and deliberately causing Mary Jane to glare back at her husband.

"Boy, you're a class act. I can't take you anywhere." Just as it seemed a domestic dispute might ensue, a young girl approached the four of them carrying a glass bowl full of tickets.

"Take a number," she announced in her little voice.

"This is Chloe. She's eight," Lucy informed them.

"Eight and three quarters," Chloe corrected her.

"We're having a drawing tonight and everyone needs a ticket. We have some prizes to give away," Lucy continued. Derek and Mary Jane dipped into the fish bowl and took tickets, which was Tim's cue to wander off. Lucy knew Tim was out of sorts for some reason. She hadn't seen him for years but could tell that he was more grumpy than usual. As he walked over to the kitchen, she followed him. Lucy took Tim's arm and pulled him gently towards some party guests. "Hey, Tim. Come over here. I want you to meet some good friends of mine."

Mary Jane and Derek turned their backs on the other mingling guests and casually strolled back towards the kitchen. Mary Jane grinned at Derek, flirtatiously. "Didn't know you were going to be here."

"Ditto. Sauvignon Blanc or Pinot Grigio?"

"Either. Just not the cheap crap I brought," whispered Mary Jane. Derek took an opened bottle of vino blanco from the fridge and filled her glass.

"Does he know?" Derek smiled gently.

"No…Probably…I don't know. Oh, who cares?"

Derek looked at her longingly. "I wanna fuck you so bad in that dress, you know that?"

"Don't be silly. This dress wouldn't fit you."

Derek coughed a laugh, almost spitting out his velvety smooth Cabernet. "You don't care if he knows, do you?" he said, still covering his mouth.

"What's he going to do? He never takes an interest in anything any more. He's a waste of space."

"So why d'you stay with him?" Derek muttered under his breath and looking around to see their conversation wasn't being overheard.

Mary Jane heaved a sigh. "God knows. Maybe I'm just a creature of habit. Anyway, it's complicated. He had a personality once. He used to be -- oh, fuck it, where's the food? I'm starving."

In the main living room of the spacious loft, Lucy introduced Tim to a sprightly couple in their seventies. "Tim. Meet Harold and Eleanor." Harold shook Tim's hand.

"Hello, Timothy. Harold Meeks. Delighted to make your acquaintance. This is my wife, Eleanor." Eleanor smiled, sheepishly.

"Hi," Tim mumbled, staring into his empty beer bottle.

"Lucy's the daughter we never had," smiled Harold. "Thinking of dating her? She's single and looking for that special someone."

Lucy rolled her eyes. "No, Harold. Tim isn't interested in dating me! Anyway, he's married. His wife's over there somewhere."

"Oops, there I go again."

"I apologize for my husband," Mrs. Meeks commiserated.

"Let me get you another Stella, Tim. By the way, Harold here worked in correctional food distribution -- whatever that means," teased Lucy, as she headed off to the kitchen to fetch another beer, leaving Tim with the quirky septuagenarians.

"Ever been in prison, Timothy?"

"Not yet."

"Well, if you had, you'd have enjoyed the culinary delights of a Fresfro meal – my old company. We delivered food to all the prison facilities in the state of Illinois."

Tim stared at the label on his beer bottle already bored with the elderly couple. "Fascinating," he muttered, sarcastically.

"Let me tell you about prison food..." Harold continued. Eleanor touched her husband's arm, deliberately interrupting him.

"Harold, Tim doesn't want to hear about prison food. I'm sorry, Tim. My husband can talk for hours about the most tedious subjects. He hates being a retiree."

"Retirement's boring, Eleanor! Got way too much time on my hands. God, I miss working for a living. What do you do to earn a crust, Timothy?" Before Tim had a chance to answer, little Chloe appeared and held up her fish bowl of tickets right under his nose.

"Take a ticket, you grumpy man!" Tim obliged the young girl just to get rid of her and tucked the ticket in his pants pocket. "Bye!" she squeaked and took off Chloe went with her remaining tickets.

"I took early retirement," Tim smirked.

"You did? A young man like you?"

"Forty-three isn't that young."

"I'm seventy-two, so you're a young man compared to me. Why did you want to do that?"

"It wasn't my idea. I got shit-canned three years back."

"Oh, dear. They lay off so many people these days for no reason." Eleanor sympathized. Tim looked around for Lucy to return with more liquid refreshment.

"Nope. I was fired -- Refusal to embrace new technology."

Lucy appeared right on cue, just catching the flow of the conversation.

"You were in printing, right?" she said, as she handed him another chilled Stella.

"Typography."

"Yes, I remember now. I think it's a dying art form. Good for you, Tim. You made a stand."

"Yeah and got kicked in the ass for it. Been unemployed ever since." There was an awkward silence as no one knew what to say to the sullen man.

"Well, I'm going to go and do some more mingling," smiled Lucy. "I have plenty of appetizers so help yourself."

In the hallway, Mary Jane and Derek stared at a large oil painting of a nude couple embracing. Derek slid his arm around Mary Jane's waist, then reached down and squeezed her butt cheek. "Mmmm…Now that's what I call art," Derek smiled. Mary Jane quickly slapped Derek's hand away as she noticed Lucy walking down the hallway towards them. Lucy pretended not to notice.

"You have a beautiful home, Lucy," Mary Jane gushed, knowing she'd been rumbled.

"Thanks. Come and join the rest of the guests, you two. I have an announcement to make."

Lucy walked with Chloe to the center of the large loft space with all the evening's party guests gathered around them. "Gather round everybody! I have an announcement to make!" The talking stopped and the guests assembled. Lucy beamed at them all. "First of all, thank you all for coming tonight to my little party. Great to see all of you could make it. Now, if you have a ticket that means you've already met Chloe. Her lucky parents are over there. That's Jasmine and Roger if you haven't met them already." A hip young couple sitting on one of the white leather sofas waved to everyone. "I've decided to give away three special gifts this evening as a thank you for being my friends and coming to my party tonight. Now, I need everyone to have their tickets ready while Chloe draws the three winning numbers."

Everyone in the room fumbled for their tickets. "Okay. The first of our three prizes tonight is...." Chloe held up small abstract painting in shades of orange and pink. "This delightful painting from my gallery by one of Chicago's most talented new artists, Emma Lafayette." Chloe pulled a ticket from the glass bowl and studied it.

"Number twelve!" Chloe shrieked.

Eleanor raised her hand. "That's me! I'm twelve!" The guests applauded as Eleanor walked up to Chloe and took the painting.

"Congratulations, Eleanor!" Lucy beamed. Eleanor held up the art work to show everyone. Harold pulled an unimpressed expression. "Second prize -- this rather wonderful sculpture I purchased on the Greek island of Mykonos. Chloe, pick another number." Lucy held up a small statue of a satyr; half man, half goat with a grossly oversized appendage. Chloe giggled, which made several guests giggle. "Don't be vulgar. It's art!" Lucy scolded them with a wink.

"Number seventeen!" Chloe shrieked at an ear shattering volume again. At the back of the room, Derek raised his ticket in the air. Mary Jane applauded loudly then dialed it down when she noticed her husband staring at her from the other side of the room. It didn't go unnoticed by Lucy who handed Derek his prize sculpture. Looking at the large erect appendage on the sculpted satyr, Derek held it up to the audience of gigglers.

"I won't say anything I might regret later," he quipped.

"Good!" Lucy announced as Derek made his way back over to Mary Jane. The smirk on her face said more than any words could. She leaned in to Derek.

"Nice dick," she mumbled.

"Thanks. Nice tits," Derek whispered back. Chloe shook the fish bowl for the final drawing.

"Okay. Our final prize is something rather special." Lucy paused. "It's a little different, so let me explain. As some of you may know, for several years I've had another passion outside of running art galleries. It's called 'channeling' and no, it has nothing to do with cable TV." A few people laughed but now she had everyone's attention. "It's way more interesting than that. I realize that it might sound a little spooky to some of you but channeling is a process of regression which allows people to discover their past lives."

"Bull hockey!" shouted Harold. "I'm glad we won the lousy picture," he said to Eleanor to the amusement of all the guests, including Lucy.

"You're not hypnotizing me, Lucy!" one of the guests joked.

"It's not really hypnotizing. More like deep meditation. Anyway, that's the prize. So, Chloe, draw a ticket." Chloe pulled out another ticket and screamed out the number with a lung busting yell.

"Thirty eight!"

Tim held up his ticket and reluctantly stepped forward to a ripple of applause. "Bad luck!" someone laughed. Mary Jane smirked at Derek as Tim handed Lucy his ticket.

"Congratulations, Tim. I'll tell you how this works later," she smiled though Tim seemed quite non-plussed as to what his prize actually was.

"Sounds…er…interesting, I guess." His underwhelming enthusiasm caused some more tittering.

"Well, that's our last prize of the evening so feel free to mingle again everybody!" Lucy announced. "We've plenty more hors d'oeuvres and lots of wine!" Mary Jane strolled over to Lucy and Tim with a refreshed wine glass in her hand.

"Tim'll make a great subject. He's relaxed most of the time these days, aren't you?" she glanced dismissively at her husband. "He'll be easy to hypnotize, Lucy."

"I need another beer," Tim huffed and left the two women to get one. Lucy turned her attention to Mary Jane.

"I haven't seen you for ages, MJ. How've you been?"

Mary Jane sighed. "Struggling. Tim got laid off three years ago and he's had his head up his ass ever since."

"That's not good. No wonder he's in a funk. Does he know you're fucking Derek?" Lucy said, directly.

Mary Jane looked dumbstruck. "Huh?"

Lucy gave her a knowing smile just as Tim returned with his third beer of the evening. If he was mad at his wife's barb he wasn't saying anything to her in public. "So, Tim. When do you want to do this regression you've just won?" Lucy asked.

"How about right now?" Tim looked at his wife with a 'fuck you' smile. Mary Jane rolled her eyes and walked off.

"Now? Really?"

Tim shrugged. "You asked."

"Well...okay then, sure."

In a dark, comfortable room away from all the hubbub of the other party guests, Lucy sat in red armchair while Tim laid down on a black leather recliner. A small table light created an intimate ambience. "Now, I want you to feel completely comfortable. Just sit back and relax. Put your feet up on that stool and close your eyes. I'm going to put on a little atmospheric music, just to help set the mood."

"What sort of mood?"

"Just relax. Take some long breaths. Those three beers you had should help." Lucy pointed a remote control at the CD player and the gentle sounds of Inca flutes started to play. A wry smile crossed Tim's face as he leaned back and closed his eyes.

"Is this bullshit, or what?" he muttered, feeling rather foolish.

"Harmless fun," Lucy reassured him.

"Yep. It's bullshit." Tim looked up at the ceiling.

"Close you eyes -- just let your mind go blank."

"I should'a had a few more beers."

"Relaxxxxxxxxx....!"

Tim lay quietly as the soothing tones floated around him. "Take a deep breath," Lucy instructed him, softly. Tim sucked in a lungful of air. "Hold it in." His chest expanded. "Now exhale slowly." Tim let the air in his lungs flow effortlessly out again. "Close your eyes -- breathe again. Hold it. Then release." With every breath, Tim was becoming noticeably more mellow. His expression softened as his body sunk into the soft leather recliner. "Good. That's better," said Lucy, softly and reassuringly.

Derek stepped out into the muggy night air on the rooftop of Lucy's condo building. Mary Jane followed him closely. "Where's your husband?"

"Lucy's giving him his prize," Mary Jane smirked. "Past life, my ass. He has no clue what he is in this one." Derek laughed. "So, Mr. Landers, guess I'll see you on Tuesday. Same time. Same place."

"Of course, Mrs. Jeffries." He wrapped his strong arms around her and pulled her in close. They kissed gently, then again and again, then more passionately before Mary Jane buried her head in his chest. She closed her eyes and hugged him tight.

Back in Lucy's study, Tim now seemed totally under. Lucy studied his calm expression. "What do you see?" Tim was very relaxed but still lucid.

"I see clouds, lots of swirling clouds. They're black and blue clouds."

"Black and blue clouds? Does that seem strange to you?"

"No."

"What else do you see?

"I don't see anything else."

"Look down."

"Nothing."

"Look at your shoes." Tim frowned. His eyelids crunched up as if trying to concentrate his vision. "Describe your shoes to me," Lucy suggested again.

Tim frowned again. "They're just shoes."

"What are they like? What color are they?"

"Brown. Brown leather boots. With long laces. Up to my ankles. My usual shoes." Lucy looked at Tim's scruffy sneakers, silently amused.

"Your usual shoes?"

"Yeah."

"Describe your clothes."

"I'm wearing my brown hounds-tooth suit. The one I always wear on weekdays."

"Hmmm…sounds very smart," Lucy said softly, looking at Tim's worn jeans and denim shirt. "Where are you?" Tim's brow furrowed.

"Don't know….dark buildings….brick walls." His breathing grew harder.

"What's happening?"

"Not sure. Horses."

"How many horses are there?"

"Two. More. Four horses. People shouting. Coppers."

"Coppers?"

Tim's expression became fixed. His soft voice abruptly changed to a hard Irish brogue. "Fucking Coppers chasing me." Tim breathed harder, quicker. Lucy looked at him with a concerned expression but her voice remained soft and calm.

"What's happening to you?"

"Bloody Coppers!"

"What city are you in?"

"London town."

"And what's your name? Can you tell me your name?"

"My name? Why?"

"Tell me your name? Who are you?"

"What name do you want?"

"Your name."

Tim didn't answer. The rhythm of his breathing slowed again and he appeared to become more relaxed. Lucy sat back in her chair.

"Never mind. Tell me -- what's the date today?"

"The 27th of September." The day calendar on Lucy's desk showed the exact same date.

"What's the year?"

"The year of our Lord, 1888. Who are you?"

"My name's Lucy."

"Liar! Don't lie to me woman!"

Tim's face reddened, his closed eyes darted rapidly beneath his lids. His lips tightened, his mouth grimaced. Lucy became concerned that her subject was obviously now in some degree of distress. "Relax, relax. Breathe deeply."

"Don't order me!"

Tim's hands clenched tight into two fists with his eyelids creased shut. His knuckles whitened. Lucy wasn't sure what was happening but she had to get control of this character that seemed to have control of her subject. "I'm sorry. I didn't mean to upset you," she quietly reassured him.

Tim's temper calmed, his breathing softened once more and Lucy breathed her own silent sigh of relief. "Okay. I'm going to bring you back into the room." Tim's breathing steadied, his eye movement less rapid. "On the count of three, when I snap my fingers, you'll open your eyes and be back in the room. Ready?" Tim's breaths became longer and deeper. Lucy leaned in towards him. "One....more awake now. Two....starting to wake up. And thr..."

Baaamm!

Chloe burst into the room, switching on the bright overhead lights, startling Lucy and causing Tim to throw his arm across his eyes. "Lucy! Everyone's looking for you!" she squealed.

"Oh, Chloe -- Not now. I'll be right there. Go back to the party." She shooed her away and quickly got up to close the door and switch the light. Tim squinted in the brightness, not sure where he was. He slowly sat up, rubbing his eyes. Lucy helped him to his feet. "I'm sorry, Tim. The session wasn't really meant to end quite that abruptly." The door swung open again. This time it was Mary Jane who wandered in looking more than a little tipsy.

"Oh...there you both are. So, who the hell were you in your previous life?" she slurred. "Don't tell me...Julius Caesar? No, wait...Albert Einstein?" Lucy ignored her, more concerned with Tim's state of well-being.

"How d'you feel, Tim?" Tim peered around the room, not sure where he was. He looked at his surroundings as if he were seeing them for the first time.

"Looks like someone just woke up from a long nap," grinned his wife. Tim looked sleepily at Lucy then turned to Mary Jane. "He looks pretty wasted, Lucy. What have you guys been doing in here?"

"Tired," Tim mumbled.

"He seems a bit unsteady on his feet," Lucy told her girlfriend, as she supported Tim's arm. "Well, we didn't exactly get a name. But he was somewhere in London and it was 1888," said Lucy, as Tim blinked and rubbed his eyes, still trying to fully snap out of it.

"Didn't think you'd get much out of him. I don't either." Mary Jane grabbed Tim's other arm and with Lucy they led him back into the kitchen. "We'd better hit the road, Lucy. Thanks for inviting us tonight. We don't get out much these days."

Out on the sidewalk, a rather intoxicated Mary Jane helped sleepy Tim into the passenger seat of their burgundy minivan. "Look, why don't I call you guys a cab?" Lucy suggested to her obviously inebriated friend. Mary Jane fumbled through her bag for her car keys.

"No, no, no! We're only a short drive away. We'll be home in ten minutes." She got in the driver's seat and slammed the door. Lucy was concerned.

"I don't think you should be driving, MJ." Tim was now snoring in the passenger seat. Mary Jane opened the car window and frowned at her friend.

"I like him like this. Maybe you should hypnotize him more often!" she hiccupped as she hit the gas pedal and the burgundy minivan shot off into the night.

CHAPTER TWO

Morning sunlight peeked through the window blinds of the bedroom on Delmar Avenue in the decidedly less salubrious Chicago neighborhood. Mary Jane rolled over and away from the glare. Her head was pounding and her throat parched. She looked at the clock on her bedside table. It was late. The bed sheet beside her was pulled back and rumpled. Wherever her husband was, he wasn't asleep in their bed, not that Mary Jane cared. She curled up and pulled the covers up over her head.

In the bathroom, Tim stood naked, staring at himself in the medicine cabinet mirror, as if he was seeing himself for the first time. He looked bright and alert. He puffed up his chest, pulled back his shoulders and stood up straight, admiring his reflection. He felt better than he had in a very long while with not a trace of a hangover. Looking around at the toiletries on display around the sink, he picked up a can of shaving foam and studied it, then examined the three blades on a Mach-3 razor. He picked up the soap, ran it under the hot water faucet and lathered his face to soften up his three-day old stubble. He picked up the razor and shaved his chin and neck but kept the three-day growth of whiskers above his lip, just trimming it into a cleaner looking moustache. He slicked back his hair and stared at his new clean-cut look in the mirror just as Mary Jane wandered in and opened a cabinet drawer looking for pills. She didn't bother to so much as even glance at her freshly groomed husband. "Where the hella the Tylenol? And why don't you feel as shitty as I do?" Tim looked her up and down as if he didn't recognize her. Mary Jane kept rummaging, finally finding what she was looking for. "There they are." She grabbed the bottle of pills and stumbled back out. Tim watched her, saying nothing.

Dressed in one of his old suits, Tim walked down the leafy sidewalk of Delmar Avenue taking in everything with a sense of awe and wonder, as if he was experiencing the sights and sounds of his neighborhood for the very first time. He appeared fascinated with the vehicles parked on the street. He watched several speed by him, stopping each time to study their streamlined contours. A plane flew overhead and he ducked. He stared up in amazement at the strange flying machine until it disappeared from view.

Tim smiled as he turned onto the main street where the traffic was busier. An eighteen-wheeler growled by making him jump back on the sidewalk though more in fascination than fear. An electronics store with its flashing neons in the window stopped him in his tracks. On display were several flat screen televisions showing the same Hollywood blockbuster movie. He watched incredulous as giant robots stomped through a downtown. For the next twenty minutes he was transfixed. Heavy rap music blasting out of a store further down distracted him and he turned his attention to the source of the loud sounds. He covered his ears as he approached the music store, giving it a wide birth.

Standing on the street corner, like someone who'd just travelled a hundred years into the future, he took in everything going on around him, invigorated by it all. He laughed out loud. He headed north where he could see more shops. Across the street, Victorian clothes in a thrift store window display caught his eye, so he crossed to take a closer look. He stared in the window at a brown hounds-tooth suit on a mannequin. He wanted it but he needed money. Feeling inside every pocket, he found a scrunched up twenty dollar bill, then went inside.

Behind a counter sat a gum-chewing, tattooed, Goth salesgirl with a pierced lip and eyebrow. She glanced up from her magazine as Tim entered, then carried on reading and chewing though Tim gave her a long, curious look which she could feel.

"Looking for anything special?" she asked in a disinterested tone.

"I want to purchase the brown suit in your window – the

hounds-tooth with the waistcoat," Tim announced in a distinctly Irish brogue. It sounded more like an order than a request.

"Huh, okay. I'll check the size," said the Goth girl, slapping down her magazine and walking over to the window. She leant into the display and started unbuttoning the brown suit on the mannequin as Tim looked at the clothes on various racks. "It's a forty two inch chest," she called out.

"Good. That's my size." He noticed a vintage cotton shirt with white clerical stud collar. On a shelf in the corner were several pairs of Victorian shoes in various states of wear and tear. He spotted a pair of brown ankle high leather shoes and checked the size. An old-fashioned cut-throat razor attracted his attention.

"Try the jacket. See if the arms are the right length." The sales girl handed him the jacket and he tried it on. He checked his appearance in a full-length mirror. It fit perfectly across the shoulders and chest though the arms were a little long.

"I'll take it. And the shirt. And the boots if they're a ten size." Tim flattened out the wrinkly twenty dollar bill and laid it on the counter.

"Okay, I'll ring you up. Let me see…that'll be $160."

Tim looked incredulous. "Don't be ridiculous, girl. I have a twenty bill and that should be more than sufficient." The Goth girl stared at him.

"Is that your real accent?"

"Why wouldn't it be?"

"I dunno. It's just so cute."

"Cute?"

"Yeah. It's cool to have a cute accent."

"Your arithmetic appears flawed. Add again, girl."

The Goth girl smiled. "You're cracking me up! Fuck, okay. Who gives a shit? Twenty bucks for everything. This is my last day here anyway."

Mary Jane sat at the kitchen table in her bathrobe, drinking coffee and reading yesterday's edition of the Chicago Tribune.

Brrrnnggg!

She had no clue who might be calling at her house. She checked her appearance in the mirror and fixed her robe, then went to answer the door. Standing on the doorstep was her husband with a large brown bag under his arm. "I don't have a key," Tim announced in his new Irish accent.

"Yes, you do. Where have you been? You never get up this early." Mary Jane ambled back into the kitchen, still feeling the effects of last night's party. Tim followed her, dumping the bag down on the kitchen table. He stared at Mary Jane with a look she'd never seen before.

"I need the sleeves taken up an inch."

"Excuse me?"

"Did I not make myself plain, woman?"

"Huh?" Mary Jane stared back at her husband with a bemused,

confused expression. "Slow down, Tim. My head's killing me this morning, so don't start ordering me about and drop the Irish accent. It's not funny, it's annoying."

"I can't go around dressed like a ragamuffin if I'm to find work," he snapped, still sounding as if he'd stepped out of a Dublin alehouse. He snatched up the morning paper, sat on a chair and started searching through the job ads. Mary Jane frowned at her husband. She'd never seen or heard him behave like this before. Her head felt like she'd been hit with a mallet and she was in no mood for Tim being all weird. She emptied out the large paper bag and its contents spilled out onto the kitchen table. She stared down at the antiquated brown suit, shirt and shoes.

"Jesus. What the hell happened to you last night? You've suddenly got money to go on a shopping spree?"

"Twenty dollars that lot cost me." Tim's eyes raced over the employment section.

"Really? And how much did you pay for the stupid Irish accent? Drop it! You don't have an Irish bone in your body." Mary Jane looked long and hard at her transformed husband. She wasn't in the mood for this. "Why are you suddenly so fascinated with wearing suits? The one you're wearing hasn't seen the light of day in fourteen years and this one's as old as the hills." Tim lowered the newspaper and looked at Mary Jane.

"Do you want me to go and out and seek a position, or not?" he snapped. Mary Jane smiled, more to herself than at her husband.

"Well, that's the first time in two years I've heard you mention *seeking a position* if that's what you wanna call it. Okay, I'll shorten the damn sleeves."

An hour later, Tim marched out of the house, striding confidently along Delmar Avenue in his freshly-tailored hounds-tooth suit with a copy of the Chicago Tribune tucked under his arm. Mary Jane watched curiously from the window. Her husband was like a new man and that concerned her. She held her cellphone to her ear. "Lucy? Hi, this is MJ. We need to talk."

Lucy Carvallo and Mary Jane sat by the window in Suzie's Coffee Shop, sipping foamy cappuccinos. "He suddenly seems so – I dunno, it's just not him," said Mary Jane to her concerned friend. Lucy smiled.

"Sounds like a good thing."

"But his whole manner...he's so arrogant now. Like he's a totally different person. And the Irish accent -- it's so weird he keeps talking like that. That regression you did...maybe it triggered something."

"It's not unusual. Some subjects wake up feeling full of life and re-energized -- freer, less encumbered but the accent thing is weird."

"And you should see the suit he bought. God knows where he got it. He never wears a suit unless it's for a wedding or a funeral but this one is more like something his grandfather might've worn."

"Come on, MJ. At least he's trying. He can't exactly afford to stroll into Barney's and get measured up for an Armani, can he? Cut the guy some slack."

"Oh, he's been slacking for years."

Lucy gave her friend a hard look. "Or maybe he's decided to change because he knows about you and Derek." Mary Jane looked down at the table. She was embarrassed. Lucy's blunt comment had hit home. "Perhaps he's trying to be more assertive -- trying to win back your affection – be more like Derek."

"Was it that obvious last night?" asked Mary Jane, sheepishly.

"Well, the ass grab was a bit of a giveaway."

"Shit."

"By the way, Derek's a player. In case you haven't figured that out already." Mary Jane looked up at Lucy, not wanting to believe her. "You should be more concerned about him than your husband."

Tim Jeffries paced along the sidewalk and stopped an elderly woman who was pushing a shopping stroller. "Excuse me, can you direct me to St. Joseph's infirmary?"

"The hospital? Take a right on Caldwell. You'll see it."

"Obliged to you, ma'am."

Ten minutes later, Tim was staring at the imposing monolithic structure of St. Joseph's Hospital. He crossed the road and headed for the entrance. As he tried to find a way into the building, he seemed confused. He couldn't figure out how to enter. The automatic double glass panels suddenly swished open for him. He smiled in wonder, then entered. Inside the expansive lobby area, outpatients and hospital staff were heading in all directions to various departments. A male nurse pushed a child patient in a wheelchair in front of Tim as he stared up at an information board. "Can I help you, sir?" smiled a Latino woman sitting at the front desk. "Do you have an appointment?"

"I'm a doctor," Tim declared.

"Oh, I'm sorry."

Tim walked away and tagged behind two men in white doctor's coats. He followed them towards the elevators. As Tim stood and waited for the elevator with several members of the public, he listened to the doctor's conversation. "See the Bulls game last night?" one of them said to the other. "What a joke that was. They should've creamed them."

Ding!

The elevator doors opened and everybody stepped in and took their spot. Various fingers hit various buttons. Tim stood silently and waited to see on which floor the doctors got off. The elevator stopped on the third floor and the two docs exited. Tim stepped out behind them and followed closely. "Excuse me, gentlemen." The doctors stopped and turned around. "Excuse me, my name is James Malone. I'm a qualified surgeon and I would like to offer my services to this infirmary. Who should I apply to?"

"This infirmary?" the doctor repeated Tim's words as he checked out his appearance. "I'm sorry, what was your name again?"

"James Malone, sir."

"HR. Next floor up. They should be able to help you."

"HR?"

"Fourth floor." The doctors walked away with amused expressions and carried on down the corridor, through two large white swing doors and disappearing from view. Tim didn't understand what they meant by 'HR'. He headed back towards the elevators as a rotund African-American nurse walked towards him. Her name tag read 'Jacinda'.

"Tim Jeffries? Cool suit, man! What are you doing here? I heard Mary Jane called in sick today. Is she okay?"

"Is who okay?"

"Your wife," Jacinda snarked, sarcastically.

"My wife?" he frowned.

"Earth to Tim. Hello? The woman you married. She lives in the same house as you. You may have seen her walking around in there for the past seven years or so."

"I'd like to offer my services," Tim announced, ignoring the nurse's question and the attached sarcasm. Jacinda stared at him.

"Uh-huh. Offering what kinda service? Doing funny accents?"

Tim straightened himself. "Don't patronize me. I'm a qualified surgeon and I can start with immediate effect."

"Now, Tim. Since when have you been a surgeon?"

"Since 1872. What is HR and where is it?"

The nurse's expression of amusement turned to one of concern. "Have you been drinking again?"

"I said, don't patronize me, woman. Can you be of assistance to me or not?"

Jacinda figured Tim had been drinking but she couldn't detect any alcohol on his breath. She'd known Mary Jane and Tim long enough to know that something was seriously up. *Maybe he'd had some kind of strange mental breakdown.* "Okay, Tim come to my office just through here and I'll go get someone to assist you." She led Tim into an admin room where she had a cubicle. "Now take a seat and I'll go find the person you need to talk to." Jacinda stepped back out into the corridor and closed the door behind her. She hurried down the hall to a wall phone and quickly dialed out.

"I'm not here right now. Please leave a message."

"Mary Jane? It's Jacinda. Your husband Tim is here acting real weird. I'm gonna take him down to ER and get him seen to. Call me as soon as you get this message." She hung up and hurried back down to the office where she'd sequestered Tim. She opened the door and entered. He was gone.

Tim walked down the corridor, checking several doors but they were all locked. He saw an Asian male nurse come out of a supply room carrying a box of bandages and walk away in the opposite direction. As the door closed slowly behind the nurse, Tim ran towards it just catching the metal handle before it closed fully. He checked that the coast was clear and ducked inside the room. The shelves were filled with boxes of surgical and medical supplies. Tim rummaged around, carefully selecting certain items, while others seemed to puzzle him. He found a box of stethoscopes, took one and put it around his neck. Finding several boxes of scalpels, he carefully examined the assorted blade lengths and made his selections. He tucked them inside his jacket pocket before moving on to a box of syringes.

Suddenly, the door opened and the same male nurse entered the supply room. He wasn't expecting to see anyone.

"See the Bulls game last night?" Tim smiled.

"Whaaa…? Who the hell….?" The nurse jumped.

"What a joke that was. They should've creamed them," Tim continued.

"Er…d'you have authorization to be in here?"

Tim smiled. "I'm a surgeon."

"Really? I've never you around here before."

"Today is my first day. Now, please excuse me." Tim moved nonchalantly towards the door. The suspicious nurse looked at Tim's dated attire and not seeing any kind of hospital identification badge on him, blocked the exit.

"You're not wearing any I.D."

"I.D?" Tim didn't understand the abbreviation.

"Do you have any hospital identification?"

"Yes, of course I do," said Tim, pushing past him and shoving open the door, walking quickly away. The male nurse walked after him along the corridor.

"What's your name?" he called out, as Tim quickened his pace.

"Tumblety. Doctor Tumblety."

Mary Jane took the elevator up to the second floor and was met by Jacinda. "Sorry to make you come in on a sick day, Mary Jane but I had to call you. I don't know what's wrong with Tim but something's up with him."

"That's okay, Jacinda. He's been acting strange all morning." They walked into one of the administrative offices and closed the door behind them.

"Alex caught him in a supply room. He thinks he was stealing stuff in there."

Mary Jane looked deeply concerned. "Why would he do that?"

"He told me he was a qualified surgeon. His exact words. Said he wanted a job here at the hospital."

"Shit. He's mentally confused."

"He's more than confused. He's fucked up, 'scuse my language."

"Where is he now?"

"We don't know. He could still be in the building for all we know."

"I'll check with security," Mary Jane replied, an air of concern creeping into her voice.

"Is he doing any kinda drugs, Mary Jane?" asked Jacinda, very concerned. "Because it was like he was hallucinating or something. He had no clue who I was, or even who you were. I mentioned your name and he was like…blank."

The admin office door opened and Alex, the male nurse, entered, looking somewhat flustered. "Oh, hey Mary Jane. I didn't know that was your husband until I told Jacinda what transpired."

"Jesus, I miss one day of work and this happens. Did you see what supplies he took? Not that it's particularly relevant but I don't even know why he would be in there in the first place."

"I saw he had a stethoscope around his neck and some of the instrument boxes had been opened," said Alex.

"We gotta find him. Is he still in the building?" asked Mary Jane, with a deep frown on her face.

"He could be anywhere now," shrugged Jacinda.

"He didn't look like anyone I recognized on the medical staff so I asked him for some I.D. Said his name was Dr. Dumbledee, I think. Something like that."

"Dr. Dumbledee? Why would he invent a name like that? This is getting weirder by the second," said Mary Jane. "He told me he was going out to get a job. Crap. Didn't think he'd come here. Well, I can only assume he's gone home. He's got nowhere else to go."

"Why don't you go back home and rest up if you're not feeling too good? I'll deal with this."

"Thanks, Jacinda. Yeah, I'll head back there and try to get to the bottom of this." Mary Jane heaved a huge sigh as her two co-workers looked on, sympathetically.

Big Bo's Brewhouse on Lexington was a dive bar that bustled at happy hour into the wee hours but it was now early afternoon and practically empty. A Lynyrd Skynyrd song was playing on the jukebox while a young blonde-haired woman in tight jeans and a white tank top sat at the bar and hummed along. She barely looked old enough to be in the place but she was consuming something considerably stronger than soda pop. A tall, tough looking woman behind the bar was drying some beer mugs as Tim walked into the dimly lit tavern. "Hey, handsome. You're looking pretty spiffed up for a joint like this. What ya drinkin'?" she barked. Tim sat himself on a barstool several seats down from the young blonde and loosened the knot in his tie.

"Bring me a stout ale."

"Aye, aye Captain!" the bartender replied obediently. She grabbed a glass and pulled a dark draft. She winked at the young blonde sitting across the counter. "Guess we're starting to attract a higher class of clientele in this fine drinking establishment," she smirked under her breath. She placed the full mug of stout on a beer mat in front of Tim and watched him down it in one. "Guess someone needed a good drink pretty bad."

"And another."

"Sir, yes sir!" the bartender chuckled, as she walked back to the beer pumps. At the far end of the bar in the shadows, sat a heavyset older man who was watching.

"Who you tryin' to impress, buddy?" He spoke at a loud enough volume to be easily heard over the strains of *Sweet Home Alabama*. Tim glanced over at him but didn't respond, which only seemed to irritate the inebriated barfly. "Darla's my girl so don't even think about hitting on her."

Darla slid another mug of beer in front of Tim and turned her attention to the baseball game on the TV above the bar. "Wanna start a tab?"

"A what?" Tim asked her, supping his second beer.

"Hey! I'm talking to you!" yelled the large man, getting up off his barstool.

"Go sit back down, Larry. This gentleman isn't bothering you." Darla looked over at Larry with a weary expression, which suggested that this was Larry's usual behavior when an unfamiliar male patron walked in. Larry ambled over towards where Tim was sitting.

"He thinks he's all that. Trying to act the tough guy, in front of my girl, huh?"

"Larry. You're being a jerk. I'm not your girl anyway," snapped Darla, arching an eyebrow. Larry wasn't listening. He was a bar bully looking for trouble and now he was heading over to where Tim was minding his own business. "This man just wants a quiet drink, Larry. Go sit back down and stick a fork in it." Darla's words didn't seem to register with the belligerent drunk who was now deliberately standing in Tim's personal space. The young blonde watched Tim as he continued to ignore Larry and calmly finished off his second beer. Larry stood his ground, so Tim turned to face him.

"And who are you?" Tim asked bluntly.

"Who am I? Who am I?" Larry shouted in Tim's face. "Who the fuck are you? This ain't your bar."

"You're right. It isn't my bar. If it were, I would have you tossed out of here."

"Don't get cute with me, you dumb Irishman," Larry slurred.

"Shut up, Larry. I'm cutting you off," snapped Darla from behind the bar.

"The name's Townsend. Frank Townsend. And I have no quarrel with you." Tim downed the last drops of his stout and banged his empty beer mug down on the bar.

"Fuck you, Irishman," sneered Larry. Tim turned back to face him.

"I don't like your tone, mister."

Larry sneered, "Who gives a..."

Smaaaaassshhh!

Tim smashed his beer mug on the corner of the bar. Glass shattered everywhere, leaving him holding just the handle with jagged glass edges sticking out.

Baaammm!

He punched what was left of the beer mug across Larry's face, slashing his flesh, ripping deep into his cheek and mouth.

"Aaaggghhhh....!"

"Jesus!" shouted Darla as Larry staggered away in agony, blood pouring from his face. Darla grabbed a baseball bat and held it two inches from Tim's face. "Get the hell outta here mister, or I'm calling the cops right now!"

Tim stood up, tightened the knot in his tie, and walked casually towards the door. As he stepped outside into the warm afternoon, he shielded his eyes from the bright sunshine then squinted as he looked up and down Lexington to get his bearings. He set off towards downtown.

"Hey, mister!" a young female voice called out after him. "Shit, it's fucking bright out here." Tim kept walking, not bothering to look back around to see the blonde from the bar trying to catch up with him. She quickened her pace and walked alongside him. "That was totally awesome back there, dude! That old guy's always mouthing off. He's a total dickwad, 'bout time someone smacked him." Tim ignored her and kept walking, locked in thought as if his mind was a million miles away. "Look, there's this real cool bar two blocks up. Wanna join me for a cold one?"

Tim glanced at her. "A cold what?" She flashed a devilish grin.

"A cold stout, as you would say!" she laughed.

"What age are you, girl?" he frowned.

"Twenty-three."

"What's your name?"

"Delilah." She smiled flirtatiously, as she linked her arm through his and tried to slow his pace. Tim eased into a more comfortable stroll and they walked together. Delilah smiled at him then snuggled her head affectionately into his shoulder.

Mary Jane parked her burgundy minivan outside her house and quickly headed to the front door. "Tim!" she yelled out as she hurried down the hallway, poking her head in every room. "Tim? Tim!" There was no sign of her husband. She stopped at the foot of the stairs and called him name again. "You up there, Tim?"

Silence.

She hurried outside to the backyard and headed towards a garden shed where Tim usually idled away his time. She pushed open the wooden slat door but there was no one inside. She stopped to think. *Where on earth could he be?* This was a man who never went anywhere and now his little solo sojourn was throwing her for a loop. A girl giggling playfully in one of the neighbor's back yards caught her ear. Then the girl screamed. Mary Jane hurried over to the fence and stood on two concrete breeze blocks to see where the sound was coming from. Two houses over, Derek was playfully spraying a garden hose over a hot young babe in a thong bikini. She was screaming in fake protest, then ran into Derek's arms for a passionate embrace. It was the last thing Mary Jane needed to witness at that moment. Her mouth tightened in a flash of anger as she quickly ducked down out of sight. Lucy's words about Tim being a player were coming back to haunt her. *What was going on in her world?* First Tim; now Derek. It was like she'd woken up in some crazy parallel universe where nothing was as it should be.

Delilah and Tim sat at the bar of the Moonlight Lounge; an old jazz club with dark corners and pockets of light. Rich, deep blue and crimson colors gave a far more intimate ambiance than the brashness of Bo's. A house musician sat at a Baldwin grand piano, tinkling the ivories to an old Bessie Smith song. Delilah looked dreamily into Tim's pale blue eyes then looked over at the stylish, white-jacketed bartender, "Hi, Chester."

"Hey, Delilah. What's happnin'? What can I get you guys?"

"Fuzzy navel. And a light," Delilah smiled coyly, as she pulled a crumpled pack of Marlboro cigarettes out of her bag.

"You know you can't smoke in here, girl."

"Shit. Just one? Please?" Delilah pouted playfully, then grinned girlishly. "Hey, Chester. I want you to meet my new friend, Frankie Townsend."

"How ya doin', Frankie?" Chester nodded.

"Porter stout!" Tim ordered, in a somewhat bombastic manner. "Make that two."

"I got something that's close," said Chester. He winked at Delilah and went off to fix their drinks. Delilah squeezed Tim's hand affectionately.

"You know the nigger?" Tim asked her, casually.

"Frankie! You mustn't say that word!" Delilah hushed him. "That's my buddy Chester."

"Chester's a nigger, isn't he?"

"He's African-American."

"Call him what you like. He's still a nigger black. Nothing wrong with that."

Delilah was not impressed with Tim's cavalier usage of the n-word but after witnessing what this man was capable of in Bo's Brewhouse, she sagely chose to quickly change the subject. "I really don't like dark beer, Frankie."

"Are you buying?" Tim snapped at her with a directness she immediately conceded to. Delilah flashed a conciliatory smile. Her eyes traced his features. There was a machismo coldness about him which she found attractive.

"So what's with the duds? How old's that suit?"

"A man is judged by the clothes he wears. Do you think someone of my standing would be seen dressed like the scallywags I've seen walking these streets?"

"Scallywags?" she laughed. "Why do you talk like that? All fancy. People don't talk like that. You an actor?"

"I'm a doctor."

Chester returned with two pints of Guinness and placed them on two beers mats in front of them. "Ugh," said Delilah, looking at the dark brews and pulling a face. Chester smiled and tossed her a matchbook. Delilah smiled back at him and took out her cigarettes again. Tim looked his female companion up and down as she lit up a Marlboro. She looked at Tim. "Do you mind if I smoke? Just one, promise."

"What business is it of mine what you do?"

By the time Tim and Delilah finally left The Moonlight Lounge and stepped outside together onto the wet sidewalk, several long hours had passed. The warm, summer rain created bright, reflective puddles of light in the evening sunshine. Several beers had lightened Tim's mood and Delilah appeared equally squiffed. As they made their way, arm in arm, along Washington Avenue, she seemed enamored by this odd man who dressed quirkily and spoke in such a peculiar manner.

After strolling by the river and through the park, the moon was high in the night sky as Delilah led Tim up the dimly lit staircase of the Fontaine apartment building on Evanston Street. It was a rundown brownstone, built in the 1920's and had certainly seen better days. Delilah was pretty hammered as she staggered her way up to the second floor. Tim smiled knowingly. Sure, he'd had several beers but he appeared far from drunk. He walked slowly behind her, watching as she tripped and fell against a neighbor's door. "Oops..!" Delilah held out her arm for Tim to grab as she slid down the door onto the hard floorboards. Tim reached out and grabbed her arm, pulling her back up to her feet. He slid his arm around her waist and steadied her as they walked down the hallway together. Neither of them noticed one of the apartment doors crack open and the spying eyes of an irritated elderly woman in her nightdress peer out at them.

Outside door number twenty-two, Delilah fumbled in her bag

for her keys as Tim stared down at the smooth skin of her slender arms and shoulders. She tossed her hair back to see more clearly in the dull light. She slotted her key in the Yale lock and twisted it. "So, Frankie baby. This is my pad." The door swung open and she fell into the room, then turned around and wrapped her arms around Tim's neck. She nestled her head into his shoulder and playfully kissed his cheek. Tim stood stoically under the door arch, seemingly indifferent to her amorous moves. Delilah leaned away and waved one of her arms towards a light switch, flicking on the overhead. She then pulled Tim inside small apartment, kicking the heavy door behind him. It slammed shut. "I've never kissed a doctor before," Delilah giggled, caressing his face. A devilish half smile flashed across Tim's face as Delilah's hands continued to fondle him.

"Is that right, my pretty trollop?" He stood quite still, studying the drunk, aroused young woman as she undid the top stud of his shirt, then slowly unfolded the knot in his tie. She kissed his neck, softly and quietly. Tim's eyes followed her as she undressed him. Delilah pulled open his shirt, kissing his chest.

"Don't make me do all the work," she purred. "Show me what a doctor can do."

"All right, my little dollymop. I'll show you what a doctor can do." His right hand flashed up and grabbed her by the throat squeezing hard around her slender neck. Tighter. Delilah struggled to breathe. His grip was powerful and the alcohol had made her weak. Her eyes widened in fear, her mouth opened in a desperate gasp for air. Now with both his hands strangling her, he crushed his thumbs into her throat. Harder and harder. Delilah's arms began to flail as she struggled for air. She punched Tim's body but he was an immovable, unstoppable force. He scrutinized her increasingly distorted expression, her eyes almost bulging out of her face. His mouth contorted into a twisted sneer as he crushed her delicate throat. Delilah's arms started to lose their energy as the life was being squeezed out of her body. Her eyes rolled back into her head as her body slumped limp.

Tim released his grip and grabbed her hair, dragging her across the room and into the bedroom. He hauled her body onto the bed and climbed on top of her, straddling her body. Delilah started to groan; she was still alive but barely conscious. Tim ripped off her tank top and pulled her blue jeans down around her ankles, tearing off her underwear. Delilah suddenly sucked in a huge lungful of air. Her back seemed to spasm as her head jerked backwards. Tim clenched his hand into a fist and smashed her face. It knocked any fight she might have had right out of her and her body lay un on the bed. The monster that had overtaken Tim Jeffries reached inside his jacket pocket and took out a small grey cloth sack. As he untied it, several razor sharp scalpel blades caught the light of the bedside lamp. Sliding out one of the surgical instruments, he deftly turned the blade towards her. Delilah moaned, slowly regaining consciousness once more but with Tim still straddling her naked body on the bed she couldn't move. She stared up in muted horror as Tim leaned over her, one hand shoving her head back to expose her bare neck, the other holding the razor edge against it. He sliced deep into her flesh, as he drew the blade across in a tearing slash, ripping through her jugular vein. Blood pumped out of her neck like a gushing geyser. Delilah gurgled a low agonizing moan. She was barely alive and slipping away fast.

Quickly, he turned his attention to her naked torso, ripping the scalpel across her stomach with a deep crisscross slash. The soft flesh of her belly opened with ease. Tim stuffed a pillow over her face to muffle any more sounds she might utter and finish her off for good. Blood began to seep heavily from the two deep wounds. Tim punched his hand inside her bloody stomach, tearing at her intestines. Delilah's muffled, muted screams of agony could still be heard underneath the pillow that Tim was still forcing down on her face. His hand ripped and twisted her guts then he yanked hard. With a manic stare in his eyes, he pulled out her bloody entrails then removed the pillow to show Delilah her own torn out guts. Her eyes widened at the horrific sight of seeing the bloody mess that was her insides as she spluttered one more low gurgled groan as the last vestiges of her being drained out of her. Finally, Delilah lay silent and lifeless. Tim stared manically at the intestinal mess in his hands and quickly mumbled a mantra-like prayer. "Holy Father Great God Lord Almighty I commit the soul of this angel of Beelzebub and witch daughter of mother Eve back to Hades from whence she came no longer shall her filthy sins bring a blight upon the great beauty of your world which you have so generously created." As her lifeless body lay on the bed, Tim's teeth clenched tight. His blood-spackled face looked around the room like a man possessed but he wasn't finished with her yet.

Mary Jane couldn't sleep. She sat up in bed and stared at the digital clock on the bedside table. It was 2:30 a.m. She reached over to switch on the lamp then got out of bed. *Where was Tim?* She slipped on her bathrobe and walked down the hallway towards the bathroom. She stopped abruptly. Someone was in the kitchen and it had better be Tim or she was calling the cops. Downstairs, drawers and cupboard doors were banging closed but it was pitch black down there. "Tim?" Mary Jane flicked on the landing light as she headed down the carpeted stairs. "Tim?" she called out again.

Silence.

Mary Jane slowed her step and stood at the foot of the stairs, peering into the darkness of the kitchen. Now she was anxious. Maybe it wasn't Tim after all. "Tim, that better be you or I'm calling the cops. And I've gotta gun!"

Silence.

Mary Jane didn't have a cell phone handy let alone a weapon. It was upstairs hidden in her chest of drawers. The noises started again. Whoever was in the kitchen was looking for something. She ducked into the den and slid open a cabinet drawer. Inside was a hammer. She grabbed it and headed towards the kitchen.

Baaaam! Baaam! Cupboard doors and drawers were being opened and slammed by someone and in the darkness. Mary Jane moved slowly towards the source of the sounds, her eyes wide and her heart beating so rapidly she could barely catch her breath. She switched on the hall light. The intruder snapped his head around and glared at her. "Ohhh...! Jesus, Tim!" Tim stared manically at her, his eyes wide. "You scared the crap out of me! What the hell is going on with you? And what are you doing in the dark?"

"There was no light. Is there anything to drink in this place?"

"For God's sake, stop talking in that stupid accent. Are you too drunk to even find the light switch?"

"Is there anything to drink in this house?"

"What the fuck were you doing at the hospital today? You freaked out my staff. Giving them fake names? What was that all about?"

"Get me a damn drink, woman!"

"In the refrigerator! You know that. And don't act like you don't know me!"

"What?"

Mary Jane could see her husband was in some strange state of emotional distress either from drink or drugs and she didn't want to antagonize him anymore. She pulled open the fridge door and handed him a beer, studying him carefully. Tim screwed off the top and gulped it down. "Booze or drugs? What is it? What have you taken?"

"I'm hungry. Do you have bread?" Tim's eyes flicked around the kitchen, as if he'd never been in the room before.

"You're really freaking me out, Tim. You need serious help." Tim swigged again belched loudly then glared at her with a coldness in his eyes that his wife had never seen before.

"Leave me be. Go back to bed." Tim finished off his beer and wiped his sleeve across his mouth. "Another!" he barked. Mary Jane just stared at him. This man bore no resemblance to the man she'd married. Maybe he'd had some type of breakdown. He looked exhausted that was for sure. Not wanting the situation to escalate, Mary Jane acquiesced to his demand, opening the fridge and handing him another bottle. She wanted to get to the bottom of Tim's extreme behavior but neither was in any mood to have a knockdown drag out argument in the wee hours of Wednesday morning.

"You'd better sleep in the other room tonight. I don't want you near me if you're going to act like an asshole," said Mary Jane as she walked back towards the stairs. "We'll talk about this in the morning when you've had time to sleep it off."

CHAPTER THREE

Mary Jane awoke at 7 a.m. to hear the bathtub running. She heaved a sigh. *What the hell was going on with her husband?* She stared up at the ceiling wondering how she was going to deal with this sudden personality disorder that was making him act so irrationally. Ever since that stupid regression he'd been acting completely out of character. *Should she call 911 and get him taken to hospital?* He wasn't going to go willingly, so then what? Have him straightjacketed out for all the neighbors to witness? She had to get Tim back to his old self of this as soon as possible where at least he was controllable.

Mary Jane got out of bed, pulled on her robe then walked down the hallway to the bathroom. She put her ear to the door and listened. The faucet's were on full blast. She paused to think -- she didn't want to confront him if he was in the bathtub. He could be in some deep, relaxed state that might do him the world of good and snap him back to normal; back to the Tim Jeffries she knew. Instead, she headed back down the hallway towards the spare room where she assumed Tim had slept. Tim's clothes were folded neatly over the armchair. She studied the brown hound's-tooth suit which he purchased the day before but her attention snapped to the white shirt, crumpled and creased in a bundle over in the corner. She picked it up and examined it. There were streaks of blood all down the front of it. Now she was concerned. She immediately reached for his jacket and rummaged through all of the pockets.

"Aghhhh! Shit!" A searing pain shot through her index finger. Something in the inside wallet pocket had sliced into her skin. She quickly stuck her bleeding finger in her mouth and sucked it to soothe the pain. Looking inside the pocket, she saw the tip of a scalpel blade protruding from the small cloth sack. "What the...?"

What on earth was he doing with a pocketful of scalpels? She figured he must have stolen them from the supply room at St. Joseph's. She'd been feeling angry about Tim's personality change but now she was feeling scared, and her finger hurt like shit. She hurried back down the hallway to her bedroom to find a Band Aid.

Back in the fragile sanctity of her bedroom with the door firmly shut, she called Lucy on her cell phone. "Lucy, this is MJ. I'm scared. You need to get over here *now*."

Lucy drove her green station wagon against the flow of rush hour traffic which was bumper to bumper heading into downtown. It was a picture perfect morning. *"It's going to be another fine day across the state today. Temperatures in Chicago should reach a high of eighty-three, dropping down to the low sixties overnight,"* said the radio deejay.

Driving along Third Avenue, Lucy eased her foot off the gas pedal as the traffic slowed. Drivers ahead of her were rubbernecking the flashing police and ambulance lights parked outside the Fontaine apartment building. Yellow police tape had cordoned off the entire front of the building and two medics were pushing a gurney through the front entrance.

Detective Mike Jacobsen was a silver-haired career veteran; a rugged, stocky man in his late fifties. He stood at the crime scene in room twenty-two with his younger partner, Pete Dubcek; taller and better looking than his grizzled boss. Inside the apartment, a forensic team carefully collected evidence around Delilah's bloody and mutilated body. Detective Jacobsen glanced around the room. Medical examiner Dr. Gilchrist, a forensic pathologist, was examining the deceased. "Do we know who she is?" Jacobsen asked Pete Dubcek, who had arrived earlier than the senior detective.

"Elizabeth Stride. Few priors for prostitution. No convictions." They both watched passively as Dr. Gilchrist shone a small light into the gaping wound in the victim's neck.

"Time of death?" Detective Jacobsen asked the doctor.

"Early hours of this morning judging by body temperature. Rigor mortis starts after three hours and there are increasing signs of that."

"Cause of death?"

Dubcek gave his more experienced partner a curious look. "Isn't it obvious?"

Dr. Gilchrist looked up and shot a look at young Dubcek. "If it's so obvious, detective why don't you tell us how she died?"

"I'd say loss of blood," Dubcek smirked. Nobody seemed amused.

"Wise ass. What else can you tell us, doc?" asked Jacobsen.

"Sharp instrument caused the wounds to the neck and torso. Could've been the same implement. Small knife or razor. These are clean cuts and they're consistent by the look of the various wounds. But I need to get the body back to the lab. I'll be able to tell you more tomorrow."

"Okay." Jacobsen tapped Dubcek on the shoulder and walked back towards the doorway. "Let's give these forensic guys room to do their thing, Dub." Jacobsen and Dubcek stopped at the entrance to the apartment to talk to a police officer. "Who found the body, Tommy?" asked Jacobsen.

"Neighbor said the door was open when she took her dog out to pee at 6 a.m. this morning. She called it in."

"If the door was still open, they must've left in a hurry. Maybe he got interrupted," said Dubcek.

"Okay, let's interview everyone in the building," Jacobsen ordered.

"I'll get on it. Neighbor reckons she can I.D. the guy. Said she gotta clear view of him."

"Good. Let's talk to her then. This character could be halfway to China by now." Dubcek walked over to a chrome specimen tray and picked up a plastic bag containing a blood-soaked internal body part. Jacobsen looked over at Dubcek studying it. "What's that -- your lunch?"

"I think it's a kidney."

"Sweet Jesus. This was some classy guy."

Another police officer called out to the two detectives. "Got a neighbor who wants to talk to you guys." An anxious elderly woman stood out in the hallway, peering into the apartment.

"Keep her outside with Tommy," Jacobsen yelled at the cop. "Hey, lady. Stay there. You can't come in here." The cop walked back over to the front door waving his arms as Jacobsen and Dubcek walked over. The old gal was agitated.

"I saw them both. They woke me up at one-thirty seven. The girl said his name - Frankie. I wrote it down. His name was Frankie."

Lucy's green station wagon pulled up outside Mary Jane's small house on Delmar Avenue and parked on the street. Mary Jane hurried out of her house and ran towards her before Lucy could even get out of her vehicle. The driver's window slid open as Mary Jane approached. "What the hell have you done to my husband, Lucy?"

"What's wrong now?"

"You need to come in and see him." Lucy switched off the car engine and got out. Mary Jane stopped her.

"Listen. You've got to reverse whatever you did. I want him back -- the way he used to be." Mary Jane looked frantic.

"Where is he?"

"Inside. I don't know who he is anymore. You gotta sit him down and hypnotize him back again and make whoever he thinks he is go away." The two women hurried along the slab path to the front door and went inside. As they headed down the hallway to the kitchen there was no sign of Tim other than a red teakettle boiling on the stovetop. "He's here somewhere," said Mary Jane, anxiously.

"Okay, MJ. Try to act calm. He doesn't need to see you all freaked out." As she finished her sentence, Tim ambled into the kitchen buttoning up a clean white shirt. He glanced at the two women then turned off the steaming kettle. "Hi, Tim. How are you?" Lucy smiled weakly.

"Is there any tea in this house?" Tim asked Mary Jane, ignoring Lucy completely and still speaking in the strong Irish brogue that he'd adopted.

"Yes, there are plenty of tea bags," Mary Jane replied, trying to keep calm. She opened a cupboard and handed him a box of Earl Grey teabags. He looked at them curiously.

"What are these?" he queried, sniffing the aromatic but peculiar small white sachets.

"Listen, Tim. Lucy needs to talk to you," Mary Jane gushed.

54

"You two need to go in the other room and then…" Lucy touched Mary Jane's shoulder and smiled, trying to calm her friend. Tim looked quizzically at Lucy.

"That's right, Tim, we need to sit down…" said Lucy.

"And, pray, who might you be?" Tim interrupted, as he tore open a tea bag and shook the leaves into a teapot. Lucy smiled nervously, visibly concerned that Tim didn't seem to have the first clue who she might be. She glanced at Mary Jane, then back at Tim.

"I'm Lucy. Lucy Carvallo. You know that. You and Mary Jane were at my party the other night. Don't you remember?" Tim poured the hot water from the teakettle into the teapot, paying scant attention to either woman.

"Lucy needs to undo whatever she did to you. Get you back to normal," Mary Jane added which seemed to amuse her husband.

"Back to normal? What are you talking about woman? I've never felt more normal in my life!"

"But it's not your life, Tim," said Lucy. "Let's go into the other room, it's quieter…" Tim put the lid on the teapot and placed an empty mug next to it.

"I have an appointment at one o'clock, so I'll be heading on shortly. Now, would one of you two women please oblige me and tell me where I might find the tea strainer in this Godforsaken house?" Mary Jane crossed her arms. It seemed that neither she nor Lucy was getting through to him.

"What appointment? You haven't had an appointment with

anyone in years. Where is it? With who?" Tim poured a small amount of milk into his empty mug and lifted the teapot, ready to pour his brewed tea.

"I have no need to discuss my business affairs with you, woman." Tim snapped. Lucy moved towards him and reached out, touching his shoulder to reassure him. He swiped her arm away.

"Keep your hands off me!" he warned, curling his fingers into two fists. Lucy pulled away from him quickly as Mary Jane pulled open a drawer and grabbed a bread knife. She pointed it at Tim.

"Now, you listen to me, Tim. I don't know what's going on with you but it has to stop. Cut this shit out or so help me God I'll use this." Tim was seething and ready to fight his knife-wielding wife, and Lucy, too if he had to. "What's your name?"

"My name is James Malone! Now put away your weaponry."

"No, that *isn't* your name! Your name is Timothy Jeffries! You're my husband!" Mary Jane kicked a chair from under the kitchen table towards him. "Sit down and let Lucy regress you."

"As I said, I have an appointment."

"Well, gee shucks! That's just gonna have to wait. Lucy is going to send you back to wherever the hell you came from."

Tim stood angrily before them. No woman was going to tell him what he was going to do. Lucy glanced over at Mary Jane. "MJ, this isn't exactly the most conducive environment for a regress..."

Baaammm! Tim's fist hit Mary Jane full in the face knocking her backwards. She slumped against a shelf of pots and pans, dropping her knife and sliding to the floor. Lucy lunged at Tim to protect her friend from further blows but Tim reacted faster and more furiously, throwing his pot of hot tea at her. The pot spilled its contents and smashed to the ground but only after scalding Lucy's arm.

Tim stormed out of the kitchen and down the hallway, grabbing his jacket along the way. He opened the front door and stormed out, slamming it shut behind him.

Lucy ran over to the sink and held her arm under the cold tap as Mary Jane slowly picked herself up off the floor, feeling her swollen cheek. "Jesus Christ. He's having a complete breakdown, Lucy!"

"Let me see your face."

"I'll be fine. You burned bad?"

"It's no big deal," said Lucy, wrapping a wet kitchen towel around her forearm.

"He's never hit me before. What am I going to do? Who has he turned into, Lucy?"

"Nothing like this has ever happened before. This is madness," said Lucy, dabbing the cut on Mary Jane's cheek with the wet towel, causing her to wince with pain.

"Sorry. You need to put some ice on that."

"I'm going to call the police."

It was almost 11 a.m. and inside Sammy's Pawn Shop on 44th Street, Tim showed an elderly man several exquisite items of jewelry. The pawnbroker closely examined the quality of the gemstones in each of the items, squinting through his jeweler's eyepiece. "Hmmm…where d'you get these?"

"Alas, they belonged to my late wife. The good Lord has her now, bless her soul," Tim said, solemnly but convincingly. The pawnbroker continued his examination of the pieces.

"Yeah, thought you might say something like that. Deeply sorry for your loss," said the pawnbroker without a trace of sincerity in his voice. "This ring is pretty nice. The emerald has good color. Ever had it appraised?"

"Not that I can recall. It belonged to my late wife's great grandmother. Been handed down over generations. I have no need for it." The elderly pawnbroker put down his eyepiece.

"Do you want to sell these items or pawn them?"

"Regretfully, I need to sell them."

"Well," he put down his eye-piece and squinted at Tim, not sure if the Irishman in the Victorian suit was playing straight with him or not. Enough people brought in items that were ill gotten gains but no one who looked as well-dressed as this guy had been in before. "Okay. I think we can do business."

Outside the downtown Chicago police headquarters, news crews and press photographers surrounded Police Chief Leo Sarcas, as he stood at a makeshift podium next to Detective Mike Jacobsen. Cameras flashed as he held a news conference. "…and due to the nature of this crime, we will be seeking the assistance of the public for any information at this point."

A reporter shouted a question. "Was this domestic violence?"

"I'll let our lead detective answer any further questions. Thank you." The Police Chief stepped back, allowing Detective Jacobsen to step into the glare of the cameras and flashlights.

"Hello, I'm Detective Mike Jacobsen. Along with Detective Pete Dubcek, I will be heading this investigation. This was a brutal attack, which led to the murder of a young woman in the early hours of this morning. We've spoken to one individual who saw the victim shortly before this crime was committed and we have a description of a person of interest. We are extremely eager to talk to this individual and I have a description. He is of average build, approximately five feet ten inches tall with reddish-brown hair and moustache. He is a very well-dressed individual, which gives him quite a distinct appearance. Do not approach this person, as we believe him to be extremely dangerous. Contact the number on your screen immediately. I will be taking no questions at this time. Thank you."

Mary Jane held an ice-pack to her cheek as she lay on the sofa in her living room, still shaken up. "My head feels like it was hit with a hammer."

"Here. Take these two Tylenol. Here's some water," said Lucy, playing nurse to her friend. Mary Jane gulped down the pills. "So, he's been this way ever since the regression. No hint of Tim has come back yet."

"No, not a glimpse of the old Tim. The Irish accent was cute at first but now he won't stop with it. It's like he doesn't know who I am. I really don't thinks he even knows my name."

Lucy listened sympathetically. "Well, he didn't seem to have any idea who I was either. I'm really sorry, MJ. This is all my fault. I've never had anyone experience anything like this before. It's like he never came out of the mental state I put him into." Lucy paused to think more about their session. "That's right – Chloe burst into the room just as I was bringing him back. That obviously interrupted him returning."

Mary Jane stared at the muted TV in her room and grabbed the remote to turn up the volume. "Look!" The local news on Channel 5 showed the tape of Detective Mike Jacobsen talking about the crime committed at the Fontaine apartments. An artist's impression of the suspect flashed on the TV screen. It looked a lot like Tim. The two women listened closely.

"We do have a first name – Frankie or Frank -- that's all we know right now. That's it. So, if anyone recognizes this individual, please contact the number on your screen as we are very keen to talk to him." Mary Jane and Lucy watched dumbstruck as the camera cut back to the local news anchor in the studio. *"Police are not releasing the name of the 26 year old female victim though she is believed to have lived at the Fontaine Apartments late last night. Let's take a look at the weather forecast now with…"*

"He had blood all over his shirt last night," Mary Jane said, wide-eyed.

60

"Now, let's not jump to any conclusions here, MJ. That sketch could be any one of thousands of men." Lucy was not buying into her friend's thought process but concerned she could well be right.

"Well, look at the timeline. It was about two-thirty when he got home with blood all over his shirt and he was real agitated. It all fits."

"No, it doesn't fit, MJ. They said his name is Frankie. He told us his name was James Malone."

"But at the hospital he said his name was Dumbledee. Doctor Dumbledee."

"Then either he's making all this shit up and screwing with everybody, or he has some kind of a temporary multiple personality disorder. The regression must've triggered something that….."

"Something that's turned him into an even bigger fucking mess than he was already."

Lucy still wasn't buying it. Truth was, she didn't want to buy into it, as that would make her culpable. "No. Tim hasn't turned into a killer overnight, MJ. That's ridiculous. If that was true…"

"… you'd be an accessory to murder."

At his desk at the Chicago Police Precinct, Detective Mike Jacobsen studied the artist's impression of the suspect's face. A plastic bag on his desk contained a receipt from the Moonlight Lounge. Pete Dubcek walked in holding two Styrofoam cups of coffee. He handed one to his partner. "Thanks, Dub."

"What'd they dig up in the lab report?"

"Nothing yet. Meanwhile, we got this." Jacobsen tossed him the plastic bag containing the receipt.

"He pay by credit card?"

"We weren't that lucky. But that sweet little piece of paper tells us the exact time they checked out of the joint." Dubcek studied the itemized receipt through the clear plastic bag. "And it would appear we he likes to drink Guinness." Jacobsen sipped his coffee and stood up. "Okay. Let's go make a house call."

Mary Jane sat in the kitchen, working on her laptop while Lucy paced the floor. She Googled the name James Malone and numerous pages of reference material appeared. "Shit. There are hundreds of James Malones."

"Well, of course there are. It will be a deceased James Malone we're looking for." Mary Jane typed the name again. Once more, pages and pages of references appeared. She puffed out her cheeks. "If we can find out who he thinks he is then maybe we can do something."

Lucy was lost in thought. "This is all my fault and only I can fix this. I've got to regress him again and bring him back into his present incarnation. That's the only way we can help him."

"Present incarnation? He's still my husband, isn't he? He just thinks he's someone else."

"No, he *is* someone else, MJ," said Lucy, emphatically.

"So where has Tim gone? Where's my husband? He hasn't just

vanished -- he's still Tim Jeffries. Explain that to me. Or is he like some zombie with someone else's brain?" Mary Jane was getting angry now. Lucy sat down beside her at the computer and took her hand.

"Tim is still Tim but it's like he's asleep inside. This older incarnation is a much stronger personality and now he has control of Tim's mind and body. This man is no longer your husband. Not until I can get him back."

"Good luck with that," snapped Mary Jane.

"What was the other name he used?" asked Lucy. "Dumbledee or something?"

"Doctor Dumbledee."

"Try that."

Mary Jane typed in the name Dumbledee. A list of odd references appeared but no people, living or dead. "There's a whole load of no one."

"Type *Doctor* Dumbledee," suggested Lucy. Mary Jane tried again adding the prefix. She squinted at the results on her laptop screen.

"There's no Dr. Dumbledee but a Doctor Tumblety came up."

"Dumbledee, Tumblety. They sound very similar. Maybe that's who he said he was. That nurse could've misheard. Is this Doctor Tumblety character deceased?"

Mary Jane read out the first reference. "A man called Tumblety, an American quack with a basic training on gross human anatomy, a splenetic hatred of women and a collection of uteruses. Ugh. That's pretty disgusting."

Lucy peered over Mary Jane's shoulder at the screen as she kept reading. "Francis Tumblety, born in Ireland, 1833. Died in Rochester, New York, May 1903."

"Tim said he was in London. It was 1888," said Lucy. "Oh, fuck! That's him!"

"Then why did he tell us his name was James Malone?"

"Keep reading."

Mary Jane's heart raced as she scrolled down the page. Lucy's eyes darted across the screen too as both women read more. "...made his career in the U.S. as a quack doctor," read Lucy.

"He was first arrested for trying to perform an abortion on a prostitute. Tumblety used many false names and disguises. He openly admitted he hated women..." Mary Jane scrolled further down revealing a picture of Dr. Francis Tumblety, mid-40s, short hair, moustache. "Look at his suit!" exclaimed Mary Jane. It was a brown hounds-tooth. "That's practically the same as the one Tim was wearing."

"It matches! It all matches!"

The two women stared at the screen but neither woman could quite believe what they were both reading -- ...*also known as The Batty Street Lodger, The Whitechapel Murderer AKA......Jack The Ripper.*

"Holy shit!"

The over-ground Loop train rattled through downtown Chicago. It was two in the afternoon and the train car was deserted except for Tim Jeffries and a young woman with spikey, magenta hair. She glanced over at Tim, more in curiosity than anything else, though he seemed more interested in the view of the downtown skyline than her. The train slowed as it entered Quincy Street station and the young woman stood up to get off. Tim stared out of the window, seemingly lost in thought. As the train came to a stop and the doors opened, the young woman stepped out onto the platform and headed towards the exit.

Within a minute she was walking out onto Quincy Street and along the sidewalk of a rather rundown neighborhood where none of the store names looked familiar. She walked past a couple of cheap black trash bags with split sides, which had spilled their messy contents out onto the broken pavement. The young woman glanced back over her shoulder and saw Tim following her. She quickened her step but Tim upped his pace. At a bus stop ahead, an elderly woman was waiting for the 3.04 to Fair Oaks to arrive. The magenta-haired young woman stopped at the bus stop and stood close to the older woman. "Been waiting long?" she asked her, hoping to engage her and deflect any approach from the stranger on the train who was approaching quickly. The old woman ignored her and shuffled forward to keep her distance.

In the brief second she turned her head away from him, Tim's hand touched the young woman's shoulder, causing her to jump. She snapped back around. "Ohhhh!"

"Pardon me, ma'am. I'm looking for a lodging house on La Salle Street. Can you direct me?"

"No! Get away from me! Fucking creep," she said, firmly. Tim's brow furrowed as he glared back at her just as the bus to Fair Oaks pulled up at the stop.

Phsssshhhhh!

The loud 'gasp' of the bus's pneumatic doors startled Tim and he took a step back. The elderly woman shuffled up the two steps and showed the driver a bus pass while the young woman stood close behind her. Tim glared at her as she boarded and took a seat by a window. Tim stared up at her magenta hair as the bus drove away. She would be easy to spot in a crowd and maybe next time she wouldn't be so rude to him.

CHAPTER FOUR

At the Moonlight Lounge on Washington Street, the happy hour crowd was yet to arrive, so it was suitably quiet for a little chat. Jacobsen and Dubcek showed Chester the police artist's charcoal sketch. He squinted at the picture and pulled a face. "Now, detective, we get so many people in this place…"

"Well, we think he was in here yesterday. He could've been with a young woman. A pretty blonde," said Jacobsen, hoping to jog Chester's memory. The bartender looked down to the ground in deep thought. He looked back up at the two detectives and shook his head.

"Nope. I can say I remember that man's face."

"The girl's name was Delilah. They were together. Know that name?"

Chester paused. "No, sir. I really can't recall anyone by that name."

Dubcek looked irritated. "You sure?"

"Yeah, I'm sure," Chester snapped back. "I might be getting on in years but I ain't senile. I don't know any chick called by the name of Delilah." Jacobsen showed Chester a small photograph of Delilah which he'd taken at her apartment. Chester shook his head again. "If she comes in here later I'll be sure to tell her you called."

"She won't be coming in today," said Detective Jacobsen. "She's busy getting an autopsy."

"Huh?" Chester stared at the two detectives. "Awww shit! You kiddin' me? Say that ain't so!" Chester was obviously upset. Jacobsen and Dubcek exchanged glances.

"What's it to you? You didn't even know her," quipped Jacobsen, sarcastically. Chester looked downcast.

"Dammit. She was an okay kid."

"So this Delilah chick you've never seen before was an okay kid?" jabbed Dubcek. "Now, isn't that a strange thing, Mike. Chester here must have a real big heart. Must be one of them sensitive types."

"Yeah, sure I seen her in here. She was a regular. I knew she was on the game. I thought you wanted to bust her for prostituting. I wasn't gonna rat her out to you guys."

"And this guy was with her?" asked Jacobsen, pointing to the police sketch again.

"Yeah, that's him."

"D'you catch his name?"

"No. Wait a moment…I think it was Frank."

"Or maybe Frankie?"

"Yeah, that's it. She called him Frankie."

"Overhear anything they were saying? They argue at all?"

"She was working him over pretty good – flirting, stroking his ego. He had a pretty strong accent."

"What sort of accent?"

"Irish, Scots? Hard to tell which. I can't never tell the difference."

"They arrive together or separately?"

"Came in together. Delilah said they'd been drinkin' down at Bo's Brewhouse. Somethin' happened down there -- had to leave real quick. Didn't say why."

A curmudgeon of a landlord led Tim down dark corridor in an old brownstone apartment building. "Some prick must've stole the bulb again." He complained, staring up at the light fixture sans bulb. He stopped at a scuffed apartment door, stuck a key in the lock and shoved the door open. He switched on a light. "Miracle. We got light." Tim followed him in. It was a small, dark, room sparsely furnished. Tim looked down at the soiled carpet. He was bemused by the antiquated air conditioning unit in the window.

"What's that?"

"Okay, so it's old. Works fine." Tim was still none the wiser as to what it was. "Okay, so this is it. You want it? Three hundred a month. Plus first and last."

"I'll take it. I'm good for the money."

"Good. I need nine hundred up front then."

"I'll pay you for one month and that's all."

"Don't jerk me around, mister. You want it or not?" glared the old guy. Tim shot him a look, then counted out fifteen twenty dollar bills. He held out the money for the old geezer to take.

"Three hundred. Here. Like I said, I'm good for it." The landlord noticed the thick wad of bills still in Tim's wallet.

"Okay, okay. I guess you are. Why a guy like you would wanna place like this beats me." He took the money and handed Tim the apartment key.

Bo's Brew house was starting to get busy when Jacobsen and Dubcek walked in. An old jukebox played a Rolling Stones song while a drunk couple danced over by the restrooms. The two detectives sat down on barstools as Darla tossed down a couple of beer mats. "Greetings, gentlemen. What's your poison?"

"I'm Detective Mike Jacobsen. This is Detective Dubcek. What's your name?"

"Er...Darla Markes. I done something?" The two detectives had her full attention.

"Were you tending bar here yesterday?"

"Yesterday and everyday."

"Recognize this woman?" asked Jacobsen, showing Darla a snap shot of Delilah.

"Yep. That's Delilah. I kicked her outta here yesterday afternoon. Is that what this is about? Is Larry okay?"

"Not sure I understand what you're saying. Who's Larry?"

"Oh, jeesh! Well, Delilah's gentleman friend didn't take kindly to one of my regulars. He gets all pissy with Larry. He got him good. Ambulance took him off to the emergency room. Cut him up real bad."

"What started it?"

"Larry was giving him shit about showing off."

"Was he?"

"I didn't think so. He was all quiet but Larry set him off. Larry gets drunk and taunts people. He had it coming, to be truthful."

"You catch this guy's name?"

"Sure, I did. Frank Townsend. He shouted it across the bar in a strong Irish accent. Everyone heard it."

Jacobsen looked at Dubcek. "Seems our Frankie had a bit of a temper on him." He turned to Darla. "Was he drunk?"

"After one beer? I doubt it."

"This Frank Townsend -- anything else about him that seemed off?"

"He was good looking guy in a old-timey suit."

"Old-timey?" Jacobsen frowned.

"Yeah, he looked like an actor who'd just come off the set or something. He was dressed like something out of a different era."

Dubcek looked at his partner. "I'll see if any film production permits were issued this week. Find out what production companies are shooting in town. He could be working as an extra or something."

Lucy checked the time. It was evening and she hadn't eaten anything all day although food was the furthest thing from her mind right now. Mary Jane's cheekbone had started to bruise up into a nice shiner and Lucy's scalded arm was still a stingy bright red. "So, what do we do now?" asked Mary Jane.

"We wait for him to come home and confront him again,"

"Or we can go to the police," Mary Jane suggested.

"And say what? Jack the Ripper is on the loose in downtown Chicago? That sounds ridiculous! They'll lock us up."

"I know it does but I don't see how we can get him to agree to another cozy regression with you. I'm not going to risk getting on the wrong end of him again. He's uncontrollably violent. We need to get real here."

"The thing is MJ, who knows if he'll even be back here tonight? He might just be gone for good."

"Or for bad."

Tim Jeffries stepped outside the LaSalle apartment building on the south side and headed towards the gaudy neon's of clubs and dives that littered the seedy neighborhood. The night was coming alive. Shadowy figures stood in doorways, drug dealers and pimps patrolled their patches in cars with dark tinted windows. Hookers in hitched up skirts and stilettoes heckled slow cruising drivers advertising their services. Tim absorbed it all as he walked further into the action. Dressed immaculately in his brown suit. white shirt and tie, he looked like a smart tourist who'd inadvertently wandered into the wrong part of town. Rap music blasted out of an underground club and just a few yards away it was drowned out by the grungy sounds of a live band. Tim's appearance didn't go unnoticed. He was a man who might have seemed out of his element but maybe he wasn't at all.

Mary Jane drove Lucy in her burgundy minivan along the state highway towards downtown. Both women were on edge. "We'll tell the police exactly what happened with the regression and everything and that we think Tim is who they're looking for."

"MJ, I think we're moving way too quickly and making some assumptions that could just be totally wrong -- a woman was murdered, Tim has blood on his shirt and you immediately think he's the killer. That's a bit of a stretch to say the least."

"You saw the police sketch of the suspect, Lucy! You saw how violent he was with us! We need to report this before I get another fist in my face."

"I'm still not sure going to the police is the right thing to do. Not yet anyway."

"That's fine for you to say. This is the man I'm married to. How would you feel about living in a house with a guy who thinks he's Jack the fucking Ripper?"

"They're not going to take us seriously, MJ. They'll think we're two crazy women."

"You got a better idea? Look, let the police find him, lock him up and then he can be regressed in a controlled environment. He'll have no way to fight his way out of jail cell."

In Mamie's Diner, around the corner from the precinct, Pete Dubcek finished off his hamburger and wiped his mouth clean with a napkin. "We know what he looks like, we know his name, we have prints and still he's not matching up to anyone we have on file."

Mike Jacobsen finished off his Michelob. "Well, I'll tell ya something, Dub. No one slices up another human being like that who hasn't had some kinda practice. He's done this before and more than once."

"That was a horrible mess today. You've been doing this longer than me. You ever see anything like that before?

"Not as clinical as that. That was surgical. He cut out her kidneys, for God's sake. This guy must've been high on something – crack, meth, bath salts…who knows what?"

"Yeah, sounds like he has some serious anger management issues if he's not jacked up on something. Someone else out there has to know this guy."

"Well, from his accent, maybe he just flew in from Ireland, done the deed and now he's back home eating a baked potato."

"There's that possibility. He's come from somewhere else to be so under the radar." Jacobsen looked tired. It'd been a long day for both men.

"You headed home?" Dubcek asked him.

"Yeah, I'm beat."

By the time the burgundy minivan pulled up at the Chicago police precinct, it was getting dark. Lucy and Mary Jane walked through the parking garage towards the entrance of the police building. "Let me do the talking, Lucy."

"Fine by me." A male figure coming from the precinct walked towards them. Mary Jane immediately recognized his face.

"Excuse me, you're the detective aren't you? The one I saw on TV today."

"No more reporters." Jacobsen walked right past them towards his car.

"Can we talk?"

"Sure, call me tomorrow. Been a long day." Jacobsen kept walking. Mary Jane was incredulous at the lead detective's attitude.

"Detective, I've got some information about that girl's murder." Jacobsen stopped wearily and turned around. The two women walked towards him. "We think we know the person who might be responsible."

"And you are?" Jacobsen sighed, more ready for bed than a conversation.

"My name is Mary Jane Jeffries. This is Lucy Carvallo. Can we go inside and make a statement?"

"Not so fast. What makes you think you know who this person is?"

"He's my husband," replied Mary Jane, matter-of-factly.

Back inside the precinct, Jacobsen took off his jacket, hung it over his chair and poured himself a stale cup of coffee, while Mary Jane and Lucy sat at his desk. "His name is Tim Jeffries and we live on Delmar Avenue," Mary Jane started.

"But he's using the names Dr. Tumblety and James Malone," Lucy interrupted.

"He's your Frankie," added Mary Jane. The lines on Jacobsen's forehead scrunched together as he gave them both a cynical frown. He looked at Lucy.

"And who are you?"

"A family friend," replied Lucy.

Jacobsen turned his attention back to Mary Jane. "You and your husband been having marital problems?"

"Well, we sure as hell are now!"

"Why would you ask her that, detective?" Lucy jumped in.

Jacobsen ignored her question, still focused on Mary Jane. "So, tell me this, Mrs. Jeffries -- who smacked you in the face?"

"He did."

"Your husband?"

"Yes."

"So this is a domestic abuse issue, isn't it?"

"No!" both the women shouted as one.

"You got into an argument. That turned into a fight. He slugs you and so you get revenge by coming here and telling me he killed some other woman. You're just wasting my time." Jacobsen was beyond irritated. He stood up, grabbed his jacket and started to put it on. Mary Jane jumped to her feet.

"No! You've got it all wrong! Tell him Lucy."

Jacobsen stood in the doorway, ready to leave. "Tell me what?"

Lucy heaved a sigh. "It started after I regressed him."

"You did what to him?"

"Hypnotic regression. It's something I do. It's how you channel past lives. I take people back to previous incarnations. I regressed her husband at a party and well, it didn't go according to plan, so…" Lucy spoke as quickly as possible to keep the detective's attention but she was fighting a losing battle. Jacobsen threw away his coffee. He wasn't buying what Lucy was selling, so Mary Jane took up the mantle.

"Let's cut to the chase – we think Lucy brought back Jack The Ripper."

"Oh, Jesus." Jacobsen wearily held his forehead in his hand. He was more than ready to go home for a good night's sleep. "Thanks for coming in, ladies. This meeting's over."

"Wait a minute!" snapped Lucy.

"Don't blow us off!" added Mary Jane.

"Y'know, you had me right up to the Jack The Ripper part."

"Look, I know that sounds a little out there," admitted Lucy.

"Oh, ya really think? Of course, that would make the guy about a hundred and seventy fucking years old." Jacobsen looked at them. He was angry and they were both in a very emotional state. "You two ladies been drinking?"

"No!" They shouted together.

"Sure you have," he said, looking at Mary Jane. "Either that or it's some lousy perfume one of you is wearing."

"Okay, so I had some Bourbon. What woman wouldn't under the circumstances?"

"Now, you two listen up. For all I know, you two could just be a couple of boozed up whacko dykes trying to get rid of the guy who's ruining your little gay love affair."

"What?" Lucy was incredulous at Jacobsen's wild accusation while Mary Jane was just plain furious.

"Are you fucking serious?" Mary Jane yelled. "I can't believe this! We come in here to help you find a killer and you accuse us of being a couple of drunk lesbians? What kind of bullshit's that?"

"Damn more feasible than your theory, Mrs. Jeffries."

"Let's get out of here, Lucy. We're wasting our damn time." Both women stormed out of Jacobsen's office but Lucy couldn't resist turning back around to fire one last passing shot.

"Detective, whether we're 'whacko dykes' or not is irrelevant.

He's still out there and he will kill again. Believe me, he will." Jacobsen waved them away dismissively.

"Thanks for the tip, ladies! I'll notify Scotland Yard!"

Outside, both women walked backed to the parking garage though Mary Jane was significantly angrier than Lucy. "Asshole! I didn't think the police would take us seriously but to insult us like that was totally unnecessary."

CHAPTER FIVE

A hooker wearing six-inch platform pumps and a mini-skirt that was two sizes too small stood on the corner of 45th and Moorpark, clutching her purse tightly. As she strutted her stuff and flipped off catcalling drivers who passed her, Tim Jeffries kept his eyes on her every move. She saw Tim coming and turned her back on the low rent traffic to face her potential new John. "How you doin'?" she said in a hard voice, as he neared. She was attractive but certainly not pretty; a street girl past her prime. Tim said nothing until he was just a few feet away.

"What price do you charge for your services?" Tim's appearance, accent and verbiage amused her. She cracked a toothy smile.

"For my services? What service you want, baby?"

"You are a prostitute, correct?"

"Well, I ain't standing out here tryin' to get a ride." She checked up and down the street, either looking out for police or her pimp. "Where's your car, baby?"

"I don't have a car," Tim answered, truthfully. The street girl was not impressed.

"No car? You from outta town then, huh?"

"You might say that. What is your price?"

"If you ain't got no car we ain't doin' business. Understand?"

"We can go to your lodgings instead."

"My lodgings? I don't think so. That's only for special customers."

"Then consider me a special customer."

"Huh." She looked back at the lack of traffic cruising now. It had been a slow night. An old jacked-up Camaro sped buy and some guy whistled at her. She ignored him and turned back to Tim. "Okay, there's an alley back there. I'll blow you for $30 or you can fuck me for $50. You gotta wear a rubber, understand?"

"Your place is better. I'll double your price."

"Okay, I guess you're too fancy to get your dick out in public, huh?"

Tim took a twenty dollar bill out of his wallet and handed it to her. "Here's a deposit." She waved him away and turned her head away from him.

"Noooo....I did not see that. Not here, baby. Let's walk." She spun on her heels and started walking away. "Put that green away.

You do not flash cash on the street, man!" Tim followed after her as she slipped down a side street. He caught up with her and they walked together. "We'll go to my place but you get fifteen minutes, tops. Understand?"

"That's fine."

"How 'bout first you give me some more of them twenty dollar bills. I wanna a bigger down payment." She winked at her new patron. Tim obliged, counting out four more bills and handing them over. She gave him another toothy grin. "Precious gonna take good care of you, baby." The long, colorful fingernail of Precious's right index finger tapped a quick text message on her cell phone to her pimp as she led Tim up the stairs to her small studio apartment. Her stiletto heels banged on the wooden stairs like a hammer whacking nails. Inside, the room was dark with a double bed, small sink and an old sofa that looked the worse for wear up against a wall. Precious sat down on the bed and took a condom from her purse. She expertly tore off the top of the wrapper. "Now, baby, I can slide it on for you or you can do it yourself. Makes no difference to Precious but you gotta wear it." Tim stood by the door and watched her.

"I don't think that will be necessary," he said, walking the short distance over to the bed.

"Oh, it's gonna be necessary, baby. Come sit. Precious gonna take real good care of you now. You in good hands." Tim sat beside her and placed his hand carefully around the nape of her neck as Precious leant over to unzip his pants. But Tim eased away from her as he gripped her neck tighter, then abruptly locked his other hand around her throat. He squeezed tight. Precious gasped, squeaking out a guttural groan. "Motherfuckerrrrr…"

She clenched her left hand into a fist and violently swung her arm upwards.

Whaaaam! Her flying fist caught Tim on the side of the head, making him reel backwards onto the bed and lose his grip. Precious sucked in a huge gulp of oxygen. She got up on her feet. "I'll cut you up bad, motherfucker! You wanna play rough with me? I'll show you what rough is all about!" Precious slipped a cutthroat razor out of her jacket as Tim swung his fist hard into her face, cutting her above her left eye. She dropped the razor and fell backwards, slumping onto the floor. Tim stood over her with both fists ready to beat her as she struggled to get up. She needed her phone and she needed her pimp.

"Strike me, would you, woman?" Grabbing her by the throat again, Tim head-butted her in the face, splitting her nose. Precious let out a groan as the blood splattered over her face. She collapsed back down again but this time Tim grabbed her and threw her on the bed. He straddled her, gripping her throat again and squeezing tight. His piercing blue eyes stared right through her. Precious's legs kicked frantically as she struggled again for air. Her eyes bulged as her mouth gaped open in a silent scream.

Tighter he gripped. Tighter.

The veins on the back of his hands were bursting - his knuckles white with the sheer force and pressure of his grip. Precious stopped kicking, her body began to go limp. Her eyes stared widely, manically, desperately clinging on to the last moments of her living being. She was gone.

As Precious lay motionless, Tim climbed off her and reached inside his jacket pocket for his surgical instruments. He quickly unfolded the small cloth sack, choosing which scalpel he needed. Ripping at her clothing to expose her torso, Tim composed himself. He was a quack doctor about to perform an ungodly act on an unwilling patient. The sharp razor tip blade of the scalpel sliced the delicate flesh of her stomach, from her navel to her pelvic bone. Blood streamed out.

Suddenly, Precious's body recoiled with a nervous death throe. Then she lay still again. Tim ripped her sliced stomach open with his hands, exposing her bloody insides. He smiled sadistically then turned his head upward in prayer. "Holy Father Great God Lord Almighty I commit the soul of this angel of Beelzebub a witch daughter of the mother Eve back to Hades from whence she came no longer shall her filthy sins bring a blight upon the great beauty of this world that you have so generously created." He slashed at her entrails with the scalpel blade. With a pair of forceps, he yanked at her uterus, ripping it free of its stomach lining. He held her uterus up in the light, like a conquering warrior holding up the spoils of war then buried his nose in her fresh innards, inhaling deeply.

Precious' eyes suddenly snapped open. She was still alive but motionless. She stared up at him, struggling to gurgle out some final words through the blood in her mouth and throat. "You….mother….fucker…"

Back on Delmar Avenue, Mary Jane returned with Lucy from their disastrous meeting with Detective Mike Jacobsen. Mary Jane called out her husband's name as they entered, hoping to high heaven he wasn't there in the house. "Tim….? Tim….!" It seemed the coast was clear for now. Mary Jane was conflicted. She wanted to resolve this crazy situation but was scared what he might do to her. The two women walked down the hallway, checking every room. There was no sign of him anywhere. "I'll check upstairs," said Mary Jane and headed up.

She checked the two bedrooms and bathroom but all was as she'd left it. She went back into her bedroom and sat down on her bed, ready to fall into it. It had been a day like no other she'd ever experienced; she was mentally exhausted and physically bruised. Mary Jane slipped off her shoes and unclasped her bracelet, then lifted the lid of her jewelry box to put it away. The box was empty – all of her jewelry was gone. "Bastard!"

She rifled through the drawers of her cabinet where she hid her grandmother's special pieces; the emerald earrings, the sapphire necklace and the beautiful diamond ring that had been handed down from generation to generation. None of the exquisite items of jewelry were there. "No!" Mary Jane, yelled out loud. Lucy ran up the stairs and into the bedroom.

"What's wrong?"

"He's taken all my jewelry! The sonofabitch!"

"Call the police, MJ. Right away."

"What's the point? To report my husband stole my jewelry? It'll be considered a 'domestic dispute' as that dickwad Jacobsen called it."

"It's insured, right?"

"It's not the money value! My grandmother's emerald ring was in there!" Mary Jane started to cry. Lucy put a comforting arm around her shoulder. "He's got money now. He's gone."

"Do you want to stay at my place tonight, MJ?"

"No, I need to stay here in case he returns. Maybe if we just knock him out, drug him. I dunno. Something."

Lucy was unsure, but seeing her friend's state of distress, reluctantly agreed. "Okay, I'll stay here tonight. I just don't think either of us will get much sleep though."

By 2 a.m. Mary Jane was sound asleep, exhausted from the day's events but Lucy was still wide awake and working frantically on her laptop, researching everything she could find about regressions. She wanted to know if there were any instances of this kind of thing happening to others. She read through the forums on spiritual websites and while she found page upon page of case studies, none of them had any evidence or suggestion that any harm could come from such sessions. She was at a loss. It was a situation she desperately wanted to remedy herself as going to the authorities had already proved to be a pointless exercise. How could she expect to be taken seriously making the outlandish claim that one of the most notorious serial killers from the 1800s was suddenly loose in Chicago? No, that was never going to fly. If Tim did kill this poor woman, how did he do it? In the same surgical manner in which Jack the Ripper killed his victims? She would have to learn more about the man Scotland Yard let slip through their hands and who had remained an enigma to this very day. But if she wanted the police to listen to her, she had better have some compelling evidence to take to them. So, to that end, Lucy spent the next several hours reading voraciously. She had to learn more about the man who terrorized the east end of London back in 1888.

Pete Dubcek sat at his desk looking over Delilah's case file as he sipped his morning coffee. The name Frank Townsend produced a long list of felons with rap sheets to match but none shared the same prints or DNA found at the scene. According to police computer records, this guy didn't even exist. Sure, he was out there somewhere, they just needed a break in the case. "Good, you're here," said Mike Jacobsen, poking his head around the corner. "Let's go."

"What's up?"

"We got another hatchet job."

"You're shitting me?" Dubcek grabbed his jacket. "Two in two days?"

At the City morgue, the torn open dead body of Precious lay on a slab. Next to her, on another table, lay the dead body of Delilah. Forensic Pathologist Frederick Gilchrist stood with Jacobsen and Dubcek looking at the two female corpses. "Okay, so here's the deal - we've got two dead women, killed within twenty four hours of each other with the same injuries caused by the same, or very similar, weapon. What do you think that suggests, detective?"

"We're looking for the same killer," surmised Jacobsen.

"That's a very high probability," the coroner agreed.

"So who do we have here?"

"Catherine Eddowes. 42 years old." Gilchrist walked around the table and over towards the dead body of Delilah. "But let's start with our first victim from yesterday, Elizabeth Stride. As you can see, her throat has been deeply gashed, and there's an abrasion of the skin about one and a quarter inches in diameter under her right brow. There's a clear-cut incision on the neck. See that? It's about six inches in length and starts here, about two and a half inches in a straight line below the angle of the jaw, three quarters of an inch over an undivided muscle, and then, becoming deeper, dividing the sheath. It's a clean cut, deviating downwards."

"And what about this latest victim?" Jacobsen was anxious to compare the two murders but Gilchrist was a stickler for detail.

"We'll get to her. I haven't finished with Ms. Stride."

"Sure, go ahead," Jacobsen replied, apologetically.

"The arteries and other blood vessels contained in the sheath were also all cut through. The incision through the tissues on the right side was more superficial, and tails off two inches below the right angle of the jaw. The deep vessels on that side were uninjured. It's evident that the hemorrhage was caused through the partial severance of the left carotid artery."

"That's what killed her?" Jacobsen asked.

"Without question."

"Jesus," said Dubcek, wincing at the severity of the wound. "What did he use to do all this?"

"A small bladed knife could have been used to do all this damage. It was done with surgical precision."

"Okay, so what about her?" Jacobsen motioned over to the lifeless body of Catherine Eddowes.

"Cause of death was the same. Her throat was cut. But she got it a lot worse. The intestines were drawn out to a large extent and placed over the right shoulder -- they were smeared over with some feculent matter. A piece of about two feet was quite detached from the body and placed between the body and the left arm, apparently by design."

"This guy's one sick fuck."

"Yes, you might say that. The cause of death was hemorrhage from the left common carotid artery. Death was immediate and the mutilations were inflicted after the fact."

"So this guy must've been covered in blood when he left her apartment. Someone must've seen that."

"Not true. There wouldn't be much blood on the murderer. Some, yes -- but not a great deal."

"You gotta be kidding me! She's been hacked to pieces."

"This person knew what they were doing. The peritoneal lining was cut through on the left side and the left kidney carefully taken out and removed. I believe the perpetrator must have had considerable knowledge of the position of the organs in the abdominal cavity and the way of removing them."

"Why would he want to do that?" asked Dubcek.

"Anyone's guess. Maybe someone needed a new kidney. Of course, he would've had to have a sterile way to transport it to whoever the hell needed it."

"What's a kidney sell for on the black market these days?" asked Dubcek.

"Well, if he wanted her kidney, why would he do all this other stuff to her? It doesn't make any sense," argued Jacobsen.

"It requires a great deal of knowledge to remove the kidney and to know where it was placed. At best, he's someone with medical training."

"And at worst?"

"He's a butcher."

"And it's the same guy?"

"I believe both of these crimes were the act of one person." Dr. Gilchrist removed his white latex gloves and threw them in the trash.

"We gotta serial killer on the loose," said Dubcek. Jacobsen scratched his head and pulled a face that suggested his partner was probably right but he didn't want to jump to any conclusions yet.

"Fuck, I hope not." Jacobsen turned to Dr. Gilchrist. "Seen anything like this before, doc?"

"Only in pictures."

"What pictures?"

"Old historic autopsy reports."

"So, this maybe guy has a history?" Jacobsen was intrigued at the possibility but Gilchrist smirked.

"I don't think so. You'll have to do better than that, detective. This was a very long time ago."

"How long?"

"Two centuries ago. Scotland Yard case history from 1888. The Whitechapel Murderer. You probably know him as Jack The Ripper."

Dubcek chuckled. "Oh well, guess it ain't him!"

"Maybe not, but as I can recall, these wounds are awfully similar."

"Seriously?" Jacobsen shook his head in disbelief.

"Could be a copycat murderer, Mike," shrugged Dubcek. Jacobsen reached inside his pocket and took out Lucy Carvallo's business card. He checked the address.

Within the hour, Detectives Jacobsen and Dubcek were walking through the doors of Lucy Carvallo's downtown art gallery. Large colorful canvases of contemporary art hung on strategically lit walls.

A young woman sat behind a desk detailing notes from whatever she was reading on her computer screen. She smiled at the two detectives "Can I help you, gentlemen?" Jacobsen flashed his badge.

"I'm Detective Mike Jacobsen. This is Detective Pete Dubcek. Is Ms. Carvallo here?"

"No, sorry, she isn't. Is there something wrong?"

"Any idea where she is, or when she might be here?"

"No, I don't. She's dealing with some emergency right now. But I can give you her number." The young woman scribbled Lucy's cell number on one of the gallery's business cards and handed it to Jacobsen. He immediately started calling it. The voicemail picked up.

"Ms. Carvallo, detective Mike Jacobsen. Hi. I need you to come down to the police precinct as soon as possible. I need to talk to you. And bring your friend. Thanks."

Pete Dubcek stood against the wall of the interview room as Lucy and Mary Jane sat po-faced opposite a sheepish Detective Jacobsen. "So, detective. Why do you suddenly want to talk to two crazy lesbians?" Lucy asked, sardonically.

"Huh?" said Pete Dubcek, totally confused by that remark. Jacobsen leaned forward in his chair.

"Okay, I know we didn't get off to the best of starts last night. I apologize. It'd been a long day."

"Guess I'm out the loop here," frowned Dubcek. "You're lesbians? Why's that's relevant?"

"No, Pete. They're not lesbians. They're not crazy either. At least I don't so. That's why we're all having this conversation." Jacobsen looked at the two women. "I'd like you to elaborate on what you were telling me the other night – so detective Dubcek here can get up to speed." Mary Jane looked at Lucy.

"Tell him about the party."

"What party?" Jacobsen asked them both.

"My party," explained Lucy. "That's where I regressed Mary Jane's husband..."

"Wait. You did what to this guy?" queried Dubcek.

"Regressed," Lucy continued. "It's like a mild state of hypnosis. I took him back to a previous life..."

Jacobsen listened attentively this time around but now it was Dubcek who was dubious. "Hold on a minute. A previous life? Are you serious?"

"Let her finish, Pete," snapped Jacobsen to his skeptical partner.

Lucy took an impatient breath. "I didn't get to bring him back to full consciousness. Not all the way. Because we were interrupted just as he was coming back."

"Coming back? Where was he coming back from?" Dubcek asked.

"From 1888," Lucy said in a flat tone to Detective Dubcek.

"And he's never been the same since," added Mary Jane. "He talks like someone from a past era. He dresses weird. He's aggressive.

He's not who he used to be."

"So now your husband is going around thinking he's Jack The Ripper?" commented Detective Jacobsen.

Dubcek had heard enough. "You've gotta be kidding me with this crap." He looked at the senior detective. "You serious, Mike? You buying this?" Jacobsen ignored his partner and focused on the two women which irritated Dubcek even more. "I don't know if you're both lesbians or not, and I don't care, but you sure sound crazy to me."

"Have you got any better leads, detective?" Mary Jane asked the irritated lawman. "My husband came home the night of the murder with a shirt covered in blood and a collection of surgical blades in his jacket pocket. He's also called himself Dr. Francis Tumblety, which I believe matches the first name of your suspect." She rummaged through her bag and pulled out a picture of Tim. She slammed it down on the desk. "And that's a pretty damn close resemblance to your suspect."

Jacobsen looked up at Pete Dubcek. "Well, Dub. She's right. We've got no other clues other than what this guy looks like and that looks like a pretty damn good match even to my jaded eyes."

"If it's anything, it's a classic copycat murder, Mike. This guy's got a Ripper fixation."

"Detective, my husband was a peaceful man. He never had a fixation on anything or anyone. He's become a monster."

"Hey, Dub. Escort Ms. Jeffries to my office and get her a cup of coffee. Give me ten minutes." That was Mary Jane's cue to get even more emotional.

"What? Why? What's going on here?" Dubcek took her by the arm and led her out. Lucy looked concerned.

"What are you doing? Why are you separating us?"

Jacobsen sat back in his chair. "I want to know that you're both telling me the same story, so I want to interview you individually."

"What? Are we suspects now?" Lucy was steamed. "I've come here to help you!"

"How did you know he would do this again so soon?"

"Because I did a little detective work on my own, detective."

"Really? Psychic detective work?"

"Study history and you'll learn the future."

"Don't patronize me, Ms. Carvallo. Tell me what you know."

"I researched the case studies of Jack the Ripper. Dr. Francis Tumblety was a suspect who used the pseudonym James Malone. They're the two names Tim Jeffries has been calling himself."

"But it doesn't explain how you knew he'd strike twice within twenty four hours."

"That's what the Ripper did. Two murders on the same day!"

"Look, I gotta agree with Detective Dubcek on this. These could well be copycat murders..."

"It's more than that..." Lucy insisted.

"But neither Francis Tumblety or James Malone are the names of our suspect."

"You have someone else?"

"We have a name, yes."

"Who?"

"You don't need to know that information. That's confidential during our on-going investigation."

"Okay, okay. I get that. Is it Frank Townsend?"

Jacobsen suddenly looked uncomfortable. That was name he had but he didn't want to admit it. He tried to keep his composure.

"Why do say that name?"

"Francis Tumblety had many aliases. Frank Townsend was one of them. That's another reason Scotland Yard never caught him."

"How d'you know so much about this Tumblety character, Ms. Carvallo?"

"Google it! It's all out there. Francis Tumblety was a con artist and a misogynist. He hated all women, even his own mother."

"So why are you so steamed up about this guy? What's it to you?"

"Listen, detective. If you want these murders to stop, and there will be more, I need to regress again and get him back to who he really is, and I can't do that until you catch him."

Detectives Dubcek and Jacobsen drove south on the Dan Ryan Expressway towards the University of Chicago. Dubcek was behind the wheel and still not sure what the purpose was for this trip. "So we're going to meet some professor?"

"Yep."

"You know, maybe you were right first time. They're two crazy lesbians."

"I don't agree he's a copycat killer. For starters, he's had zero medical training so he isn't capable of suddenly having the skills of a surgeon."

"Well, they're convinced they've brought Jack the Ripper back to life and now it sounds like you've jumped on that bandwagon, too. It's bullshit, Mike. I can't believe you're going along with it."

"He could still be our guy. Put it this way, Dub. We need to be up to speed on the history of this Ripper shit before this damn Lucy Carvallo woman makes us look like a couple of dumb shits."

Crime historian and law professor William Clementis pulled various files from a beaten up leather satchel. Jacobsen and Dubcek sat in the tattered but comfortable leather armchairs in the distinguished educator's study. "I must admit I was rather surprised to get your phone call, detective. But then this case has baffled criminologists for years."

"Thanks for seeing us at such short notice, professor. You seem to be the authority on the subject and me and Dub here would like to know more."

"Any particular reason for this sudden visit?"

"No," the two detectives said in unison.

"Well, delighted to be of assistance." The professor laid out various photocopied documents and crime scene photographs on his large mahogany desk. Dubcek and Jacobsen studied each artifact as the professor gave them a brief history lesson. "For years, no one knew who Jack The Ripper was. There were dozens of suspects, hundreds of theories. Then, in 1995, a Ripper enthusiast obtained permission to search Scotland Yard's archives. He came across a conveniently forgotten letter tucked away in an obscure place. In it, Chief Inspector Littlechild of the Yard named a Dr. Francis Tumblety, this con man and quack doctor, as the prime suspect. Seems they just couldn't catch him. He was too smart. Always one step ahead of them. Plus, this Tumblety fellow had numerous aliases - Frank Townsend, James Malone...Tumblety kept evading capture even though they even brought him in for questioning on one occasion. You see, Tumblety was simply smarter than they were -- always had a back up plan -- kept a rented apartment in Liverpool so he had somewhere to run back to and a direct route by ship back to New York when things got hot. Tumblety was the Ripper all right and Scotland Yard knew it. They just didn't want anyone else to know it. He was a huge embarrassment to them because this man was the most terrifying criminal of the century and they could not nail any of these murders on him. Jack The Ripper was the scourge of London town and everyone was terrified. Scotland Yard had to protect their reputation so they buried the evidence.

"Wow, that's quite the history lesson but what can you tell us about his victims?"

"Well, there were five women with whom the Ripper was connected directly. A few others, too but they were not confirmed Ripper victims, though some attest to the fact that there could be more. But these five women are his for sure. Mary Ann Nichols, Annie Chapman. Elizabeth Stride…"

"What?" Jacobsen sat up in his chair. "Elizabeth Stride?"

"Yes, victim number three."

Jacobsen stood up and took a closer look at a copy of the original autopsy report. "How is that spelt?" He checked the spelling of the name. It was identical to their first murder victim. "How about that," said Jacobsen with an understated calmness. Dubcek pulled a face.

"She was murdered the same day as the Ripper's fourth victim, Catherine Eddowes."

"Okay, now that's freaky."

"Why's that. Detective?"

"No, I was just thinking how freaky he murdered again the same day," replied Jacobsen, not willing to spill the beans about their case.

"Quite," the professor continued, "Murdered both women on the same day. September 30th, 1888."

"That was yesterday."

"Well…yes. Give or take a hundred and thirty years," professor Clementis smiled. "Quite a coincidence, I suppose."

"More than you can imagine," mumbled Dubcek.

"When did he kill again?" Jacobsen asked the professor.

"Good question. Many claim the Ripper was responsible for the Whitechapel murder on October 3rd. 1888. Of course, there was considerable speculation as the..."

"What was her name?" Dubcek interrupted.

"Well, that was a bit of a problem. They never knew who the poor victim was because they never found her head."

Jacobsen sat back in his chair, dumbfounded. Both detectives realized this was far more than a simple copycat murderer on the loose. This man was finding women with identical names to the Ripper's original victims and murdering on the same date. As creepy as this was, it at least gave them a clue as to what, or who, might be his next victim, unless they could find him beforehand.

"How many more women did the Ripper murder?"

"There was just one other, on October 9th."

"What was her name?"

"Mary Jane Kelly."

"Well, I guess we'd better round up every Mary Jane Kelly we can find and keep them locked them up until October 10th."

"Excuse me?" Professor Clementis seem confused.

"Just a little police joke, professor," smiled Jacobsen.

Lucy sat at her computer reading more about the case studies of Jack The Ripper's victims while Mary Jane sat at the kitchen counter, picking at a plate of food. "Take a break, Lucy. You haven't eaten anything today."

"I want to know what the Ripper did next. If we know his next move we could lay a trap to catch him."

"But Jack the Ripper was never caught."

Lucy started reading about Jack the Ripper's last victim. Her mouth opened in shock as she reads the name 'Mary Jane Kelly'. She stared at the autopsy photo of a disfigured face and mutilated body. She took a deep breath as she looked up to see her friend place her dinner plate in the sink. "Hey, MJ?" Lucy said, trying to keep her voice steady. "What was your maiden name?" Mary Jane walked back over and frowned at Lucy.

"Odd question to ask. Kelly. Mary Jane Kelly. Why?"

Lucy faked a smile. "Just curious. I've always known you as Mary Jane Jeffries." Lucy's heart was racing a mile a minute. She couldn't believe the names matched.

"Why did you want to know that, Lucy?"

"No reason," Lucy lied.

"Bullshit. What are you looking at?" Mary Jane rushed over to see what was on Lucy's computer screen. Lucy slammed her laptop shut. "Let me see, Lucy!" Mary Jane elbowed Lucy aside and opened the laptop. She paused as she read, her face turned ghost white. "Mary Jane Kelly. Murdered October 9th, 1888. Oh, my God, Lucy. He's going to murder me!"

Mary Jane hurriedly packed her overnight bag in her bedroom. She opened a drawer in her bedside table and took out the handgun she kept there. She tucked it in her purse. Under where it had been kept was an old greeting card with a single, elegant red rose on the front. Mary Jane opened it and a photograph of her and Tim on their wedding day slipped out. The two of them looked so happy. How far they had come from that day seven years ago. She read what Tim had written inside: *To the perfect wife, happy one year anniversary, love Tim.* She felt like ripping it up but stopped herself. Her eyes started to well up and she wiped away a tear, then closed the card and put it back in the drawer.

Honk! Outside Mary Jane's house, Lucy sat parked outside in her station wagon waiting for her friend to come down with her things. She looked up impatiently at the bedroom window then looked around anxiously for any sign of Tim Jeffries returning home. The discovery that Mary Jane shared the name of the Ripper's last victim had spooked her out and she wanted to get them both away from her house as soon as possible.

Up in the bedroom, Mary Jane's phone rang. She answered it quickly with one hand and grabbed a small suitcase with the other. "I'll be right down."

"Good. I miss you," said a familiar male voice on the other end of the line she certainly wasn't expecting to hear

"Derek?"

"Hey, baby."

"Derek. It's over."

"Huh?"

"I'm not one of your little bimbos, you lying jerk." She hung up and took off downstairs. Derek's call had made her even more flustered. He was the very last person she needed to talk to at that moment. She ran out of the house towards Lucy's car and got in.

"Got everything you need?"

"I think so."

"It's better you stay with me from now on. Just to be safe." Mary Jane didn't answer. "You okay?"

"Derek just called." Lucy said nothing. She started the engine and drove away towards the safety of her downtown condo. Lucy figured Mary Jane had enough to deal with without her piling on about an extra-marital affair that was really none of her business anyway. "It's over. I finished it," said Mary Jane, breaking the silence. Lucy changed the subject.

"Detective Jacobsen contacted me again. He wants to see us first thing tomorrow morning."

"Did you tell him my name is on the death list?" The fear in Mary Jane's voice was palpable.

"No."

"What? Why not?" Mary Jane snapped. "I need police protection, Lucy!"

"Because they're still having a hard time buying into the whole storyline of Tim's regression. I don't want to try and to tell them something they simply won't believe."

"So you're not going to tell them that the Ripper's last victim had the same name as me?"

"Well, we don't know the names of the other two women that were murdered the other day and we don't know for sure that Tim was even responsible."

Mary Jane was incredulous at Lucy seeming to back track. "What do you want to do then? Wait around until October 9th for Tim to come after me, slit my throat and rip my guts out and *then* go to the cops? Is that what you want, Lucy? Is it?" she yelled at the top of her lungs.

Lucy kept her eyes on the road and her hands on the wheel. "Okay, we'll tell Detective Jacobsen first thing."

CHAPTER SIX

On the south side of Chicago in a small, grubby bathroom, Tim Jeffries was stripped to waist and cleaning his incriminating surgical instruments in the white porcelain sink. He carefully towel dried each one, wrapped them in cloth and slid them back inside his jacket pocket hanging on door peg. His miniature armory was prepped and ready for another clinical attack. He cupped his hands under the running old water and splashed his face. Letting the water drop off his face, he stared at his reflection in the mirrored medicine cabinet. He looked long and hard with no visible trace of emotion; just lost in thought. *Who was he? Where was he? Did he know? Did he care?*

He walked back into the bedroom and over to a bookshelf but there were no books; just a row of clear glass jars containing human internal organs. It was a morbid collection. Tim stared at the jar containing the fresh kidney of Catherine Eddowes. He studied it closely then calmly ran his hand through his hair.

Jacobsen and Dubcek walked into the precinct at 8 a.m. and Lucy and Mary Jane were waiting for them. The two women quickly stood up when they saw the two detectives. "Glad you ladies are both here," said Jacobsen as Pete Dubcek walked on ahead. "We gotta big fucking problem."

He followed Dubcek who led them all along a corridor and down a flight of stairs into the basement. He opened an over-sized heavy security door and all four of them entered. They were now in a command center for the state of Illinois. A giant-sized computer generated map of Chicago was up on the far wall. Two police officers sat at computers, monitoring the city.

"Sit down. Both of you," Jacobsen ordered. The two women obeyed. Jacobsen took a breath. He looked at Dubcek, then back at Lucy and Mary Jane. "Now something very strange is going on. There are way too many bizarre coincidences going on here with our suspect -- whether or not he's your husband -- I can't find a logical explanation to any of this but I'm trying to keep an open mind."

"What were the names of the two women who were murdered?" Lucy asked the detectives.

"We're not at liberty to divulge the names of the deceased at this stage of the investigation," replied Dubcek, sounding every bit like a pre-recorded, politically correct public servant.

"Is that so? Well, we're done here then." Lucy shot back as she and Mary Jane stood up to leave.

"No more help from the crazy lesbos," added Mary Jane.

"Their names were Elizabeth Stride and Catherine Eddowes," blurted out Jacobsen.

"Oh, no!" Mary Jane gasped. Suddenly sobbing uncontrollably.

"Shit!" said Lucy, as she tried comforting her distraught companion. Jacobsen and Dubcek exchanged confused looks.

"Why is she so upset?" Jacobsen asked.

"Because she's next."

In the briefing room at the Chicago Police precinct, Mike Jacobsen stood before several rows of police officers. Pete Dubcek stood beside him as they addressed the uniformed audience. "This is what he looks like -- reddish-brown hair, pale blue eyes. Five feet ten inches tall. Thin build, forty-two years of age," said Jacobsen, referring to a photograph of Tim provided by Mary Jane. A quiet mumbling went around the room. "But this guy sticks out in a crowd like a black guy on a swim team."

No one laughed. An African-American cop in the front row rolled his eyes at Jacobsen's tacky analogy. Jacobsen noted the officer's reaction. "No, I'm serious, Dave. This guy dresses like a Victorian gent in a distinctive brown hound's-tooth three-piece suit. He's so damn arrogant, he's not even trying to hide or blend in with a crowd. Now, we have it on great authority..." Jacobsen glanced over at his partner. "...that this guy will kill again this Wednesday."

"We gotta name?" a voice at the back of the room called out.

"His real name is Timothy Jeffries but he's using all sorts of aliases. Dub...."

"Frank Townsend, James Malone, Doctor Francis Tumblety. They're the names witnesses have heard him use. He also has a very pronounced Irish accent."

"This guy operates on the south side," added Jacobsen, "And he has his own ideas about reducing the proliferation of prostitution in the area. He is extremely dangerous so proceed with caution. We need to bring this guy in ASAP. Okay, that's all gentlemen. Be careful out there."

Jacobsen and Dubcek cruised through the south side of Chicago in their Crown Victoria clocking everyone on the street. Lucy's station wagon followed them. The detectives wanted the two women along to make a positive I.D. and no one was more qualified than Mary Jane. It was 11 a.m. and the neighborhood was already alive with action. The usual local characters were going about their business, young and old. Any one of them looked like the stereotypical suspects you see in any given TV crime series. It was the perfect backdrop for the man they were looking for; he'd stick out like a sore thumb, for sure. Dubcek was behind the wheel, while Jacobsen kept an open line on his cell phone directly to Mary Jane. Behind the detective's vehicle in the station wagon, Mary Jane held her cell phone tight to her ear. Her nerves were like jelly -- she felt like an accident waiting to happen. According to the history books, the date of her violent execution at the hands of her husband was five days away. The question was, could she stop history from repeating itself?

The radio in the detectives' Crown Victoria was set on the police frequency so they could hear all messages incoming from the other police vehicles cruising the area. This could be a long day but with un-marked police cruisers scouting the area they tried to stay positive. It was a sorry collection of low-lifes of various ethnicities so a white guy in a sharp Victorian suit should be an easy spot, unless he had gone local in his attire. *"Suspect I.D.'d on Lexington at Fair Oaks,"* said a voice on the radio.

"Let's go," said Jacobsen to Dubcek and to Mary Jane on the other end of the line. Dubcek slammed his foot down on gas and took a hard right onto Lexington Avenue.

"Stay close, Lucy," said Mary Jane, passing on Jacobsen's instruction. Lucy did her best to follow the detectives but the Crown Vic was moving fast now. She veered right and followed as best she could. The two vehicles sped along the wide road. Dubcek took a quick left on 4th Avenue and continued at speed towards Fair Oaks. The green station wagon started to lose them so Lucy gunned it and eventually caught up with them.

As they reached the corner of Lexington and Fair Oaks, two police cruisers had lights flashing at a newsstand. Two cops on the sidewalk had their handguns drawn and pointed at a willowy looking guy in a brown suit who was frozen to the spot with his hands above his head. The man looked terrified; his hands trembling. "Suspect at two o'clock," said Jacobsen in his cell to Mary Jane. She looked wide-eyed to see more closely on the busy sidewalk where the crowds had scattered. She stared hard at the man they'd apprehended.

"No."

"No?" Jacobsen repeated.

"Not him."

"You sure?"

"Positive."

"Shit," mumbled Jacobsen. Dubcek picked up the radio handset.

"Wrong guy. Stand down. Repeat. Stand down. Release the subject." The police officers lowered their weapons and approached the still shaken man in the brown suit.

"Suspect sighted. Brown suit. 21st and Grossman," said another voice on the police radio.

"Let's go!" Jacobsen barked again. The Crown Vic took off and swerved around the next corner followed by Lucy's green station wagon. A dark gray Ford Mustang with no visible police markings pulled out in front of the Crown Vic and the three vehicles sped to the new location, several blocks away.

At 21st and Grossman, a middle-aged man in a pair of khakis and a brown leather jacket was handcuffed and pressed up against a store window. A police officer had a firm grip on him as he shoved the man's face sideways onto the glass front. The three vehicles slowed down so all the occupants could get a closer look at this new suspicious individual. "Jesus Christ," groaned Jacobsen. "Does that look like a brown suit to you, Dub?"

"Not even close."

"Nope, not even close," Mary Jane repeated over the phone to Jacobsen as she locked eyes on the suspect and saw immediately it wasn't her husband. Jacobsen grabbed the radio mic.

"Suspect is wearing a brown hound's-tooth suit. Not khakis, not a brown leather jacket – a brown hound's-tooth suit. Out." He glanced at Dubcek. "Let's keep cruising."

For the next hour, the black Crown Victoria and the station wagon trolled the south side. The four of them knew the consequence of not finding Tim Jeffries. If the timeline which he seemed to be working to stayed consistent, it would mean another dead body showing up tomorrow and this one would be missing a head.

Tim Jeffries crossed at the light on Caxton Street and walked towards the Tulip Café. He was still figuring out his new surroundings but right now he was hungry and thirsty. Dressed in his distinctive brown suit, he was an easy target for anyone looking for him. The Crown Victoria stopped at the red light as Tim crossed the street. Lucy and Mary Jane were right behind. There was their man – in plain sight.

"Fuck! That's gotta be him!" yelled Jacobsen to Dubcek and to Mary Jane over the phone. Mary Jane's head turned every which way till she lasered in on him.

"Yes! That's Tim!" she shouted back. The lights changed to

green just as Dubcek and Jacobsen jumped out of their car and ran across the street to where Tim was walking stealthily along the sidewalk. A row of cars stuck behind Lucy's station wagon started honking their horns for her to move through the green light but they weren't budging. The cacophony of sound was enough to make Tim glance back, only to see the two detectives running furiously towards him. That was his cue to take off along the busy sidewalk. The chase was on.

Lucy backed up as best she could to get enough room in front of her to maneuver around the Crown Victoria still parked in the middle of the road. "Can you see them?" she shouted to Mary Jane who was clambering over the back of her passenger seat to get a better view of the pursuit.

"I think all three of them ran up that side alley."

Tim was moving quickly but with no idea where he was going. He didn't know the streets and alleys. He cut down a gap between two large buildings but there was only a brick wall ahead and it was blocking his escape. The two detectives were closing in. They had him now. He was trapped. There was no easy way out unless he could scale that wall. Filled with adrenalin, he ran at it and attempted a leap at it but it was way too high. He wasn't going anywhere anytime soon. Jacobsen and Dubcek slowed down and caught their breath as they saw Tim had nowhere to go now. Their chests were heaving, gasping for oxygen as they moved in on their suspect. Jacobsen grabbed the firearm tucked in his shoulder holster. He wasn't taking any chances. "Freeze! You're under arrest!" Jacobsen barked. But Tim wasn't going to oblige them quite so easily. He looked skyward and saw a black wrought iron fire escape on the side of one of the buildings. Crouching to get some spring in his legs, he leapt up and grabbed the last step of the stairwell and hauled himself upwards.

"Freeze or I'll shoot!" yelled Jacobsen but Tim was already ascending rapidly up the first flight of iron stairs. Dubcek took a run and jumped up at the fire escape, managing to grab enough of it to haul himself onto it but Tim was now two flights ahead of him. Jacobsen aimed his Glock skywards and fired a shot into the air.

Bang!

Tim ignored the warning. He was now at the top of the fire escape. The only door into the building was bolted shut. He had nowhere to go and Dubcek was getting closer with every passing second.

Crrrraaash! Tim smashed his elbow into the opaque window and shattered the pane. He clambered through as quickly and carefully as he could to avoid the jagged glass edges that could slice him as cleanly as his scalpels. Just as Dubcek reached the top of the stairwell, Tim disappeared into the building. Not willing to risk ripping himself to shreds attempting to climb through the shattered window, Dubcek hammered on the bolted door. No one answered. He impatiently kicked out the rest of the jagged window glass so he could climb through more easily.

Inside, the building was just an old disused warehouse with heavy machinery covered in dirt and dust. Dubcek could hear the sound of echoey footsteps racing down a stairwell. He ran over to an set of metal bannisters and looked down to see Tim in full flight heading towards the front entrance of the building where he could escape onto the busy sidewalk. He chased down after him, reaching for the weapon in his shoulder holster as he ran. Tim was moving in and out of the sweating detective's line of sight. Dubcek stopped on the first floor and took aim. "Freeze!" Tim kept running. Dubcek aimed at Tim's legs, hoping to bring him down.

Bang…!!!

"Fuck!" yelled Dubcek, as his shot missed it's target. *Bang…!!!* A second shot fired wide. Tim unbolted the double front doors then disappeared out into the street. Dubcek followed as fast as he could but Tim was gone.

Lucy saw a parking space and swerved in to snag it. She slammed the gear stick into park and got out. "I saw him come out of that building."

"No, Lucy!" shouted Mary Jane. Lucy slammed the driver's door behind her and took off running down the sidewalk after Tim. Mary Jane panicked at being left alone with Tim in the vicinity. She locked the car doors and ducked down out of sight.

An elderly homeless woman pushing a shopping cart didn't see Lucy running towards her. Her entire worldly belongings were piled high as she ambled along mumbling to herself. Lucy abruptly skipped to her right to avoid the vagrant and smashed into Pete Dubcek running behind her. *Baaammm!*

"Shit!"

"Uhhhhh!" The two fell hard on the pavement. The elderly lady pushed past them, giving them both a disapproving look. Wherever Tim was now, he was out of sight. "Damn it!" Dubcek got up and dusted himself down. Lucy sat on the ground rubbing her head. "Your job was to stay with Mrs. Jeffries and I.D. the suspect."

"I'm sorry. I didn't know you were chasing him."

"This is police work. This is what we do!"

Mike Jacobsen caught up with his partner, puffing hard. "Lose him?"

"Yep."

"Fuck!"

For the next four hours the Crown Vic and the station wagon cruised the south side. There were no more sightings of Tim and no more false alarms either from any of the police cruisers. The two detectives were becoming frustrated and in the car behind them, Lucy and Mary Jane were getting increasingly anxious. "He's not going to get you, Mary Jane. We'll just keep you protected until September 9th passes, or until the police get him behind bars."

Pete Dubcek was still livid. "I could've caught up with the freak if that damn Carvallo woman hadn't – we gotta get them off this case now, Mike. We know what he looks like. They've done their part."

"We need to contact every hotel, motel and boarding house in the inner city. Everyone who ran a classified ad for a room -- check it."

"That could take weeks. If this stupid Ripper timeline theory plays out as you seem to think, then someone's going to get decapitated in the next twenty-four hours."

"We'll never know that until we find a headless body."

"This is Chicago, Mike. We could find several. Shit. I'm getting hungry. I need to eat," he moaned.

"Let's grab lunch over at Louie's place. It's close."

The four of them sat together in a booth at Louie's Café on Fenshaw Street. It was almost two-thirty and Pete Dubcek was still irritable. Jacobsen made a finger map of the Chicago area on the table. "Right now, he's somewhere in here," he pointed. "So we have cars and beat cops all over it. If we don't find him before dark then finding him becomes considerably more difficult. He could easily skip town now he has money to travel."

Lucy dug down into her bag and pulled out an iPad. She tapped the Maps application and a grid of Chicago appeared. "Use this, detective. It's a little more accurate," she smiled. Jacobsen ignored the dig and looked at the graphic map. "In 1888, Scotland Yard were closing in on him so he fled London and went to Liverpool, a port town in the north of England. I think that's where he's headed."

"Liverpool?" sneered Dubcek.

"There's more than one Liverpool, detective."

Jacobsen thumbed his chin. "But according to history, the Ripper killed someone on this day back in 1888. He's not leaving till he's killed his next victim."

"Maybe she's already been killed," said Mary Jane. It was an obvious thought which none of the others had considered. Dubcek stared at the menu, hungry and tired.

"That's true, detective. It could just be a question of when you find the body. He could be on his way to Liverpool by now."

Dubcek slammed down the menu. "Damn, Mike! Who's leading this investigation -- you or her? He's off to jolly old fucking England now? Gimme a break!"

Jacobson shot a look at Dubcek. "Leave your ego out of this, Dub. Clementis backs up everything she's telling us."

Lucy continued: "Liverpool. That's where he's headed. Liverpool was where he took the ship back to New York. That's why Scotland Yard never found him.

"That doesn't make any sense!" Dubcek held up his hands. "This is Illinois, not England. If he's trying to get back to New York, he's already on the right side of the Atlantic. He doesn't need a ship to get him there from here. So why would he want to get to Liverpool first? He's already here in the U.S. Liverpool's five thousand miles from here in another fucking country."

Lucy scrolled her fingers across the tablet screen, moving the map southwards. "Look closer, detective," said Lucy, pointing to a town marked on the map. All four of them looked down. Her finger was directly on a town south west of Chicago called Liverpool.

"No shit. Liverpool, Illinois. Two hundred miles southwest of here," said Jacobsen, staring straight at Dubcek. "He'll probably take the Greyhound." Dubcek was still dismissive.

"Aww, c'mon! There's gotta be a Liverpool in every state in North America."

"There's eight actually," said Lucy. "Illinois, New York, Pennsylvania, Texas, Alabama, Indiana, Louisiana and West Virginia." Jacobsen gave his partner a sarcastic smile. But Dubcek wasn't finished yet.

"And it could be any one of your eight Liverpools."

"It'll be Liverpool, Illinois," Lucy said, emphatically.

"Look, even if your Liverpool theory has merit, that's two hundred miles away. You think this guy is going to go to those lengths to copy this Ripper character?"

"Why not? He's done it to the letter so far," said Mary Jane.

"But this is America. That happened back in jolly old England," argued Dubcek. Lucy tapped the iPad screen and a map of England appeared. She glanced up at the unconvinced detective. "That's as maybe, detective but look at this." Lucy held up the tablet for both detectives to see.

"See the difference between London and Liverpool, England? Two hundred miles. Same distance as Chicago to Liverpool, Illinois."

All eyes were now on the unbelieving Dubcek.

"Y'know, I've never even heard of Liverpool, Illinois," grouched Dubcek at Jacobsen. Mary Jane leaned across the table.

"Don't let your lousy geographical knowledge hinder this investigation any longer, Detective Dubcek," snarked Mary Jane.

"What if little Lucy here is wrong? What then, Mike?" said Dubcek, shooting daggers at Mary Jane.

"Then it's my ass on the line, Dub and if I get canned, you'll get my job. But what if she's right and we did nothing?"

Dubcek sat back in his eat. "I don't want us to waste valuable time on a wild goose chase. I just wanna get this freak locked up before here hacks up his wife."

That was too much for Mary Jane to take. She held her head and sobbed. Lucy scowled at Dubcek. "Guess you skipped that sensitivity training class, detective." Dubcek looked at Jacobsen and shrugged. Mary Jane wiped her eyes as Lucy put a comforting arm around her.

"I can't take this any more, Lucy. I'm...I'm just exhausted. I just want to go home. This is all a nightmare."

"You can't do that, MJ. You know that. We can't let you out of our sight until he's captured."

"We've already got officers on every damn street corner on high alert," Jacobsen said, trying to reassure her. "If he's in that vicinity, he's caged in. If Lucy's right and we know he's gonna be on a bus heading to Liverpool, we can stake out every Greyhound stop in Chicago and nail the sonofabitch."

"But he could already be on that bus," suggested Lucy.

"I doubt it. Me and Dub are to go back to the precinct and map this out. We need to get everyone up to speed on this and get them on track."

"Take me home, Lucy," said an emotionally spent Mary Jane.

Jacobsen nodded. "Okay, take her to a safe place and meet us at the station as soon as you can. I need your knowledge of the Ripper's history."

Lucy drove Mary Jane back to her downtown loft. "You just need to sleep, MJ. This is getting exhausting and you really don't need to be dealing with this." Mary Jane sat silently in the passenger seat, not talking.

Back in the control center at the precinct, Lucy stood with the two detectives looking at a giant map of Chicago on the wall. Several police techies sat behind computer monitors. Lights on the map flashed intermittently, indicating various trouble stops around town. Jacobsen went over to one of the techies. "Hey, Dougan, can you show the Greyhound bus routes? I want to see which buses go to Liverpool." A young guy with dark-rimmed glasses hit his keyboard with rapid fire fingering.

"No Greyhound buses go to Liverpool. That place is tiny."

"Huh. What's the closest stop?"

"Peoria."

"How far is that from Liverpool?"

"Let's see…thirty four miles," said Dougan. Jacobsen scratched his head. He looked at Lucy.

"So, you're saying he's going to Liverpool when, in fact, he really wants to get to New York."

"Right."

"Except he can't get to New York from Liverpool because you can't get anywhere from there."

"True. That does appear to be the case."

"Then I don't get it."

"He's repeating everything the Ripper did and, so far, he's done it to the same timeline. It's like he's hot-wired to repeat everything that happened in 1888. Eventually he took a ship to New York. So, using that same logic, if he's not here in Chicago then he'll be trying to get to Liverpool now."

"I say we keep looking on the south side," said Dubcek. "If this guy's just stepped out of 1888 he won't even know where to get on a Greyhound bus. This is Chicago, not London.

"Maybe he *thinks* it's London," offered up Jacobsen, not sounding as certain as before but wanting to bolster Lucy's argument. He was savvy enough to know that as bizarre and horrific as these coincidences were, it was all just too weird. And Dubcek was punching holes in Lucy's Ripper/Tumblety scenario.

"His every move is based on everything that happened back in

1888. Can't you see that?" Lucy stated adamantly. Dubcek had a cynical grin on his face.

"I gotta question, Ms. Carvallo. Tell me this – why would he be trying to leave town when the history books tell us he committed his final murder six days from now on October 9th in the same area where he killed the other women?"

"That's an extremely pertinent question, Dub. I'm glad you're bringing an element of logic into your argument." Jacobsen waited on Lucy for an equally pertinent answer. She thought for a moment.

"Tumblety rented a place in Liverpool, which he would retreat to and hide out when the trail got too hot in London. I believe that's where he's headed because he's going to try and rent a place there."

"That won't be easy in a town that small," said Jacobsen.

"Correct. But he doesn't know that yet."

"According to Dougan here, he has to get to Peoria first," added Jacobsen, helping to answer Dubcek's question.

"So, you're telling me he'll turn back around and come back to Chicago in time to kill Mary Jane Kelly on October 9th?" Dubcek asked both Lucy and Jacobsen.

"That would fit the history books," she replied. Dubcek pursed his lips, not convinced Tim Jeffries would stick so rigidly to this path of action.

"You got any better ideas, Dub? No, didn't think so. Dougan?

"Yep?"

"When does the next bus leave Chicago for Peoria?" Dougan's

fingers went to work at lightning speed again.

"It departed twenty eight minutes ago."

"Well, shit! Let's get after it."

It was six minutes after seven in the evening and a Greyhound bus screamed down Interstate 55 South heading towards Peoria. Towards the rear in the half full bus sat Tim Jeffries. The seat beside him was empty and the only passenger behind him was a young woman in her twenties. She was wearing white cotton skirt with cowgirl boots and a pink cut off t-shirt that revealed her tanned, flat stomach. Her dirty, straggly blonde hair was scrunched up as her head rested wearily against the window. She had a rucksack beside her and she was having trouble staying awake. Tim glanced back around at her. The sun was low in the sky and the other passengers on the bus were either reading or sleeping as the bus engine droned monotonously. The pretty blonde yawned and her eyes closed as she drifted off to sleep. Tim glanced back at her a second time then checked that no one was observing him. He got up and moved three rows back to sit next to her. Her head rested against her raised arm. Tim looked down at her bare stomach and belly piercing. "Your parents don't mind you dressing like that?" The young woman blinked and snapped awake.

"Huh? Wha...? Like what?"

"Like a dollymop," Tim said through gritted teeth.

"A what?" she said, indignantly.

"You heard me -- like a trollop."

She sat up, annoyed. "No one asked you to sit here, mister. Go back to where you were sitting or I'll call the driver."

"I'll sit where I want to sit."

"So will I then." She grabbed her rucksack and stood up. Tim shoved her back down again. "Get off me, you jerk! You can't touch me." Tim's hand grabbed her throat and squeezed tight. She gasped for air. He pinned her in her seat while squeezing his grip tighter and tighter. Her eyes widened as Tim cut off her air supply. Several seats ahead, a young man listened to music on his iPod, his head gently nodding to the beat, blissfully unaware of the struggle going on behind him.

Detective Pete Dubcek was gunning the Crown Vic Ford down Interstate 55 behind two speeding police cruisers with their lights flashing and sirens wailing. The convoy flew past the traffic, which switched lanes hastily to get out of their way. The bus Tim was on was forty-five minutes away from Peoria and the chasing convoy was gaining on it, albeit still a good ten miles behind. "There's no guarantee he's gonna be on this bus. You know that?" said Dubcek as he gripped the wheel with the assuredness of a professional driver. Lucy leaned over the back seat and looked at the speedometer.

"Wow. We're going over a hundred."

"Yeah, can't you go any faster, Dub?" snarked Jacobsen.

On the back seats of the Greyhound bus, Tim's thumbs pressed hard against the jugular vein in the young girl's throat, tightening his vice-like grip. She couldn't breathe let alone utter any sound to summon help. No one on the bus had any idea what was happening behind them. Her pretty brown eyes started to roll back in her head as the monster Tim had become choked the last breath of life out of her. Her limp body slumped down on the seat beside him. Tim pulled a serrated kitchen knife from inside his jacket and started cutting through the flesh of her neck. Blood started to spill out of her, over her clothes, over the seat, over Tim's butchering hand. Quietly, under his breath, he mumbled as he sawed through her. "Holy Father Great God Lord Almighty I commit the soul of this angel of Beelzebub..."

The Crown Vic was gaining ground on the Greyhound. It was in visual distance now. "There it is!" announced Dubcek.

"Shit, we did better than I thought," smiled Jacobsen. "Way to go, Dub." Way up ahead, the Greyhound bus was traveling at sixty miles per hour on the inside lane. The two police cars up ahead seemed to switch into hyper drive as they suddenly closed in on their target. Both police vehicles swung into the middle lane so the bus driver could see their lights flashing and hear their sirens. The Crown Vic followed closed behind. "We'll get this sonofabitch before that bus ever gets to Peoria's city limits," snapped Jacobsen.

As all three police vehicles closed in on the Greyhound, it started to slow. The leading cop car sped ahead of the bus and slowed down, forcing the bus driver to decelerate even more. The lead car signaled to the bus driver to take the next exit then led the Greyhound off the Interstate. The second cop car stayed beside the bus to chaperone it while the Crown Vic stayed behind to observe the big picture.

The bus drove into the parking lot of a rest area and stopped as the three police vehicles drove around to the front of the bus, facing its front and passenger door. Four armed officers got out of their vehicles and took protective positions behind their cruiser doors with their guns drawn. They were prepared to use deadly force if they had to. Jacobsen looked at Lucy sitting in back seat. "As soon as you give us a positive I.D. we'll move in."

"Okay," said Lucy, looking anxiously at the dramatic scene unfolding before her eyes. Jacobsen flipped the trunk open and got out of the Crown Vic. He walked back and grabbed a bullhorn.

"Driver, open the door! I want every passenger to get off the bus, one at a time, hands in the air! Hands in the air!"

Pssshhh! The pneumatic doors of the bus swished opened. The first passenger to step out of the bus was an elderly man, moving slowly and struggling to walk with his arms raised. "Sir, please move over to the right of the bus! Stay where we can see you!" The elderly man did as he was told. "Okay, sir. You can drop your hands now."

The second passenger to step out of the bus was a Latino soldier wearing army fatigues. The third passenger was a college student. "Okay, okay, I'll pay my fucking fare!" he yelled at the police officers. "Jesus, you people are damn Nazis!"

"Move to the right and stand with the others!" barked Jacobsen. Two middle-aged woman got off the bus next, loaded up with grocery bags. That seemed to be it. Everyone waited, guns drawn and pointed at the door of the bus. "Anyone else on board, driver?" The bus driver stepped off the bus, his hands in the air.

"No, sir! That's everybody!"

Dubcek looked at Lucy with a told-you-so expression. Jacobsen nodded to a police sergeant who signaled to two police officers wearing Kevlar body armor to advance. The two officers approached the Greyhound, guns in hand and arms extended, aiming directly into the bus. They boarded slowly. The first officer crouched low, peering under the rows of seats to see if anyone was hiding. He nodded to his fellow cop, giving him the okay to board and follow behind him.

Jacobsen, Dubcek and Lucy waited silently beside the Crown Vic while the officers disappeared inside the Greyhound. All was deadly quiet. Two cops waited with the disembarked passengers who were all clueless as to what was happening but all remained compliant, even the angry student. The two officers stepped back off the bus. "All clear!" shouted the lead officer.

"Fuck!" Jacobsen blurted out, angrily. Dubcek heard something on his police radio. He leaned his head back into the Crown Vic and listened to the police dispatcher. *"Officers in pursuit of Greyhound bus en route to Peoria."* Dubcek looked over at Jacobsen and Lucy.

"God dammit! We stopped the wrong bus!"

A Greyhound bus bound for Peoria sped along the interstate with a state trooper in pursuit. Its lights were flashing and Tim could hear the siren. He glanced out the window then grabbed the dead girl's rucksack and walked forward past the disinterested passengers to the front of the bus. The heavy set bus driver could see Tim approaching in his rear view mirror. "Return to your seat, sir while the vehicle is moving."

"Stop the bus! I want to get out!" Tim demanded as he stood behind the driver. All the passengers on the bus were now very much awake and alert. "Sit down, jackass!" one passenger bellowed from halfway back.

"I'm not permitted to stop, sir. Please return to your seat!" repeated the driver. Tim pulled out the kitchen knife. It was still bloody.

"I said I want to get off of this vehicle!" Tim yelled. The driver quickly reached down and pulled out a gun as he steered with his left hand, he aimed the handgun at Tim with the other.

"And I said return to your...." *Thwaack!!* Tim swung back the rucksack and smashed it across the driver's head. The driver managed to hold onto the steering wheel but dropped the gun.

Bang...!!!

The bus swerved in and out of its lane. Passengers screamed and dove for cover. All of them were all now very alert and in a state of total panic, fearing for their lives. The driver managed to grab the wheel again with both hands but his head was cut and bleeding. The

128

pursuing state trooper slammed on his brakes to avoid a collision. "Go sit down, you bully!" a elderly female passenger nearest to Tim yelled. He ignored her and swung again at the driver. *Thwaack!!* The rucksack crashed against his head causing the bus to swerve all over the road again.

"Stop this bus!" yelled Tim, taking a third swing at the driver's battered head. Blood was now pouring down his face and he was having trouble seeing. *Thwaaack!!* The rucksack burst open and the dead girl's head fell into the driver's lap.

"Aaaagghhh!!"

He slammed his foot on the brake pedal and the Greyhound screeched to a stop. The state trooper following slammed his brakes too and swerved out of control, spinning out on the interstate and colliding with a truck in the passing lane. The bus driver opened the doors and Tim leapt off. It was almost dark now. He jumped over the concrete wall that ran along the hard shoulder and landed in some brush. Then off he ran, disappearing into the night.

Detectives Jacobsen and Dubcek were speeding back down Interstate 55 with Lucy in the back seat. Dubcek gunned the gas as they topped a hundred again with the two police cruisers ahead of them. The three vehicles sped towards Peoria, lights flashing and sirens wailing once more. Jacobsen got a phone call. He listened intently. "Awww…shit!" He turned to Dubcek. "They found victim number three on the bus. He decapitated her."

"Oh, God!" said Lucy. Dubcek look shocked as he kept his eyes on the road ahead. Jacobsen listened to the caller some more. "Okay, Lou. Jesus Christ, I don't believe this guy. On our way." He ended the call and turned to Lucy. "He beat up the bus driver and got off the bus. They've lost him."

"Well, we know where he's heading even if it's on foot."

Tim cut through a moonlit cornfield, glancing back to check he wasn't being followed. The interstate was way behind him in the distance now but he could still hear the rumbling of traffic. He slowed down to catch his breath. He was a safe distance from civilization though he had to figure out where he was. He looked up at the stars in the fading blue sky to get some kind of bearing. The tall corn hid him from view but it was disorientating. He had to find somewhere to hide out for the night. He kept walking until the sound of freeway traffic dissolved away to be replaced by the call of a lonely owl and crickets. He kept walking until he came to a clearing, only he knew for sure where he was headed now but if could find a path it might lead him to a road and he could journey on to his intended destination. He felt a deep rumble in the ground. There was a fluttering sound in the distance and it was getting nearer. Seemingly out of nowhere, dazzling halogen searchlights were beaming down on the cornfield behind him from the sky. The cornhusks swirled under the downdraft of helicopter blades spinning. Tim ran for all he was worth. The roar of the chopper's engine grew louder and louder as its searchlights scanned the field. Tim ran harder but now he was in clear view. He needed the protection and cover of the cornfield but it was too dangerous to head back there now. As he turned back briefly to see where the bright spotlights were now searching, he figured he could make it to the densely wooded area a few hundred yards ahead. That'd give him enough cover until they passed. He ran for his life but the chopper was now heading towards him. The halogens were proving useful inasmuch as they illuminated the trees ahead but now they were almost on him. Faster and faster he ran, he was only fifty yards from escaping into the woods but now the noise of the chopper suddenly became deafeningly loud. It seemed almost upon him. Blinding halogens hit him hard and stayed on him. Thirty yards and he would be under tree cover. The chopper flew lower and louder as it zoomed in on its target suspect. Tim was panicked but the woods looked brighter than daylight now and he could see his way into them clearly.

"Uhhh…" Tim was plunged into darkness as the halogens averted their dazzling glare and the chopper swerved upwards, skimming over the trees to avoid them. He was safe for now but couldn't see anything further than a few feet in front of him. Carefully, he made his way through the undergrowth and ducked down, wondering where the chopper might reappear next. Laying flat and breathing hard, he waited. He needed to recover. His stamina was seriously sapped. He listened as the rotary engine of the chopper faded into the night. No one could find him now. Tim lay still, his breathing slowed as beads of sweat trickled down his forehead. He would wait, laying low until his pursuers moved on.

A light in the distance caught the edge of a Birch tree and Tim's eyes widened. A second light caught the leaves close by. He listened for any noises to gauge the distance of this new disturbance. A dog barked, then a second dog. Whoever it was, they were deep in the woods but less than a hundred yards away by the sound of things. He had a choice -- stay still and silent, or move on now. The barking dogs were getting louder and nearer. He stayed still, lying flat on his stomach. Maybe they had picked up the scent of the girl on the rucksack he was still carrying. He grabbed it and swung back his arm, tossing it away from his hidden position as far as he could. The rucksack hit a tree branch and fell no more than ten feet from him. It made enough noise to agitate the approaching hounds even more. They were barking non-stop now and straining to be unleashed.

Tim could lay still no more. He got up to make a run for it. Now he was surrounded my moving flashlights. The dogs were after him, leaping through the brush. There were two, three, four German shepherds chasing and barking. Tim had no idea where he was going but his legs were moving as fast as they could. The dogs were coming at him too fast. He leapt up and grabbed a tree branch, hauling himself upwards. The dogs could see him now but he was off the ground. The powerful German Shepherds arrived in unison and stood barking up at him. He was safe from their bites but he was going nowhere. Police flashlights shone on the dogs then on Tim.

They had their man.

CHAPTER SEVEN

Lucy gently touched the shoulder of a sleeping Mary Jane. "Hey, you. How did you sleep?" Mary Jane jolted awake as if suddenly waking from a nightmare.

"Uhhh!"

"I brought you some orange juice." Lucy handed the glass to her sleepy friend. Mary Jane gladly took it and sat up in the bed to sip it. She looked like Hell.

"Oh, thanks....what time is it?"

"Nine thirty. How do you feel?"

"Like shit. What happened yesterday?"

"They got him. Tim's in custody." Lucy sat down on the end of the bed. Mary Jane felt a huge sense of relief.

"Oh, Thank God! Now what happens?"

"They found a third victim. He cut off her head."

"Oh, no! Just exactly as it happened to the day." Mary Jane held her face in her hands. "What should we do?"

"Detective Jacobsen wants us both to go down to the station and make an identification and statement."

"Okay. I'll get dressed."

Tim looked out from behind the iron bars of a holding cell at the Chicago Police Department. His steely blue eyes stared manically as two police officers walked down the corridor of locked up drunks and bums to check on him. Tim listened to their conversation as they approached his cell. "...and that's how it happened."

"Just like that?"

"Yup. Just like that. One, two, three..." *Click!* The officer snapped his thumb and finger and Tim's tense expression immediately relaxed. His manic stare softened and his anger abruptly turned to fear. He looked around his cell, confused.

"Excuse me. Excuse me!" Tim called out in his distinctive mid-western accent. The two cops stopped and looked back at him.

"What?" asked one of the officers, disdainfully.

"Why am I here? Did I do something wrong?" The two cops looked at each other and laughed.

"Did you do something wrong? You sure did, buddy."

"What? Tell me what! Why am I here?"

"You ran a red, pal. Ha ha!" The two cops walked away down the line of holding cells. For the first time, Tim looked frightened.

"Hey! Seriously! Why am I in here?! What did I do?!"

Lucy drove Mary Jane through downtown in her to the police precinct. Both women were locked in thought and not conversing. Mary Jane finally broke the silence. "What's going to happen to him now, Lucy?"

"He murdered three women. What do you think?"

"This is all so unreal. Tim has never even raised his voice about anything in seven years of marriage."

"I'm so sorry, MJ. It's all my stupid, damn fault. I'll never forgive myself."

"Stop apologizing, Lucy! What's done is done. I know I've lost my husband but you and I both know I'd already lost him. Our marriage was a disaster. I'd been seeing Derek for almost nine months."

"D'you think Tim knew about it?"

"Probably. But he never said anything. It's like he knew I'd lost all respect for him. He just went downhill after he lost his job. I guess I wasn't sympathetic. I wanted him to get up and dust himself down and go out there and just doing something else. Anything! He just used to mope about the house feeling sorry for himself."

"Well, it can be tough out there. That was hard for him. He had a good job and they're not so easy to find any more."

"I know...don't make me feel worse, Lucy. Yeah...I was pretty hard on him. I feel awful about it now. I mean...this is beyond anything I could ever imagine happening."

"His self worth must've been at an all-time low when I stupidly regressed him. This personality that's overtaken him – it was just too strong for him to handle, I guess. Shit. It couldn't have happened at a worse time for the poor guy."

"Like I said, it's done now. I feel dreadful about this. I feel it's my fault, too Lucy. Fuck, I was screwing around with Derek when I should've been being more sympathetic."

Tim sat handcuffed in an interrogation room with detectives Jacobsen and Dubcek sitting across from him. Tim's demeanor seemed different. His whole body language had changed. He looked a sad, lonely figured with his hands cuffed behind his back and a far cry from the man who had eluded the police on his killing spree. "Can you please tell me what this is all about?" Tim asked, without a trace of an Irish brogue.

"Who's Francis Tumblety?" asked the lead detective, ignoring Tim's question.

"Tumble who?"

"Tumblety."

"I don't know."

"Who's Frank Townsend?"

"Never heard of him."

"James Malone?"

"Look, I don't know any of these people. Never heard of any of them. I'm not part of any gang if that's what you're getting at. I've never had any association with any of them. Ever! I would really like to talk to my wife if that's possible."

"We need to establish a few things first. Tell us who you are."

"Again?"

"Yes."

"My name is Timothy Michael Jeffries." Tim spoke firmly but softly in his normal voice. "I live at forty seven Delmar Avenue, with my wife Mary Jane."

"Do you know why you're here?"

"No! I don't! Unless you tell me, how the hell am I supposed to know?" Tim raised his voice in frustration. "Obviously I'm under arrest for something, in which case I would at least like to know the charges or have a conversation with either my wife or a lawyer. I'd also like to know why I'm dressed like this. These aren't my clothes."

"All in good time," said Jacobsen, looking at him with a furrowed brow.

"Look, I really don't know what's going on, detective. I don't even remember anyone arresting me."

"This guy's hilarious," chuckled Dubcek.

"You have no clue why you're here?" Jacobsen asked him wearing a jaundiced expression.

"Look -- all I know is I was talking to a woman named Lucy at a party."

"Lucy who? Where and when?"

"Lucy Carvallo. She has an art gallery downtown. She's a friend of my wife's, Mary Jane. It was just a few hours ago. Did I get drunk and do something stupid?"

"Nice touch," smiled Dubcek. Jacobsen sat forward in his chair.

"A few hours ago?"

"That's right, detective."

"What was the date of the party?"

"It was today -- September 28th."

"Today's Wednesday, October 3rd."

"Bullshit! That's not possible!" Tim looked perplexed.

"Five days, buddy," said Dubcek, growing weary of Tim's unconvincing answers. "Let's just say you've been a little busy since your little night out." Tim's expression became more troubled.

"Why won't you tell me what happened? Did I do something bad?"

"You could say that."

"Come on! Stop playing games, detective. What are the charges? It's my right to know why I've been arrested."

"You've been arrested on suspicion of three counts of murder in the first degree." The two detectives waited for a reaction. Tim stared blankly back at them. His mouth opened but no words came out. His eyes searched them both as if he couldn't believe what he was hearing. Jacobsen and Dubcek remained silent waiting for a verbal response.

"That's...that's ridiculous! Ridiculous! Three counts?" Tim blurted with an incredulous tone in his voice. "Oh, come on! This is some kinda set up here! This is bullshit! I need to speak to my wife!

"You are the prime and only suspect," Jacobsen told him. "Are you prepared to take a polygraph?"

"A lie detector? Absolutely! Whatever it takes to prove I'm innocent of this crap."

Jacobsen stood up to leave. Dubcek followed then looked back at Tim sitting cuffed in the chair. "Make yourself comfortable." The two detectives left Tim alone in the room as the heavy metal door slammed shut.

Jacobsen and Dubcek stood with Lucy and Mary Jane in a dark room. The four of them observed Tim in the interrogation room through two-way glass. Tim was oblivious to their prying eyes. Detective Dubcek chewed on a toothpick. "Well, either he's one helluva actor or he's totally nuts."

"Says he was at a party and now he's here. Everything in between is a blank. Doesn't know why he's been arrested. He's acting like nothing ever happened," said Jacobsen.

"Well, that's why he was never caught," Lucy smiled, "Francis Tumblety was a well-skilled con artist."

"We caught him though. Scotland Yard didn't," snarked Dubcek to Lucy. Jacobsen scratched his cheek as he pondered the situation.

"Your husband have any history of mental illness, Mrs. Jeffries? Any depression... Bi-polar disorder or schizophrenia. Anything at all?"

"Not in the slightest," Mary Jane answered, honestly. "He's always been so boringly normal. But what if he's back to being Tim again?"

"He could be working an angle but I'm not so sure. He told us his name was Tim Jeffries."

"What? How would he know that unless…?" Lucy interrupted. "It means he's come out of his regressive state! Francis Tumblety didn't know he was inside the mind of Tim Jeffries. Something must've snapped him back to this incarnation."

"Oh, thank God!" said a relieved Mary Jane. "It's over!" She looked at her husband through the glass with an affection in her eyes for the first time in a very long time.

"Pretty damn convenient if you ask me," snapped Dubcek. "Easy to say you don't remember after ripping three people to pieces." Lucy didn't agree with the cynical Dubcek.

"It could be true, detective. That was the last time he was himself. It's like he's been asleep for five days."

Dubcek smirked. "Yeah, well let's see what a judge says about that this afternoon when he's arraigned."

"I need to talk to him," gushed Mary Jane.

"Not yet, Mrs. Jeffries."

"Why not, Mike?" Dubcek asked his partner. "Let's she what she gets out of him." Lucy looked deeply troubled.

"If Tim is back to being himself and back to reality, he'll have absolutely no idea what he's done since the party."

"But he's back and it's over. That's all that matters," said Mary Jane. "My husband would never have committed these atrocious crimes. He's not a violent person."

"Oh, really?" Dubcek looked her straight in the eye. "I've got three mutilated corpses that would say otherwise if they still had the ability to speak. We've also got a collection of female organs in glass jars and now a severed head. I'd say that's pretty good evidence he *is* violent, don'tcha think?"

"Well, he never was in our marriage. That's all I'm saying. What will happen now?" Mary Jane asked the two detectives.

"He'll be arraigned in court this afternoon," said Jacobsen.

"What does that mean?"

"He'll go before a judge and he'll have to verify his identity and the charges will be read out against him. A trial date will also be set. He's going to need an attorney or a public defender. Or, if your husband prefers, he can represent himself though I would strongly advise against that."

"I want to talk to my husband," Mary Jane demanded. "Surely, I can do that, can't I? Doesn't he have the right to talk to me?" Jacobsen and Dubcek exchanged glances. Jacobsen nodded. Dubcek walked Mary Jane out into the hallway where a police officer met her and opened the door of the interrogation room. Tim strained his head to look around. The police officer entered accompanied by Mary Jane. Tim was still cuffed but pleased to see her.

"Oh, thank God. Mary Jane, get me outta here."

"Hi, Tim. How are you feeling?"

"What's going on? This is like some really fucked up dream or something. They're telling me I murdered three people. It's ridiculous! You gotta get me out." Mary Jane sat down and looked sorrowfully at her husband. For the first time in a long while, she pitied him. Her bottom lip quivered as she struggled to keep back tears.

"It's not going to be that simple, Tim."

"What the hell happened? They're telling me five days have passed since the party! That's crazy."

"It's not crazy. It's true."

"Five days? Have I been unconscious all that time or something? I mean – I'm not a murderer. I've been a lifelong pacifist, for God's sake! You know that. Tell them that! Tell them about the party!"

"Lucy's party is where it all went strange. After the regression you became violent. You hit me and attacked Lucy."

"What? Oh, come on! I don't remember doing that."

"But you did. You did some terrible things."

"What's the matter with you, Mary Jane? You believe them?"

"Look, at the party you were regressed by Lucy. Remember the ticket? The prize? You won. You recall all that, don't you?"

"Sure, I do. At Lucy Carvallo's house. One minute I'm relaxing on her couch and seconds later, here I am in handcuffs, sitting in a

Goddamn police cell under arrest. This is bullshit!"

"Lucy regressed you and you channeled this person -- this previous life. Someone called Francis Tumblety." Mary Jane wondered if the name might trigger something in her husband. She looked for any sign of recognition in Tim's eyes but he just seemed even more bewildered.

"Who is this Tumblety guy?"

"Doctor Francis Tumblety. That's who you became after the regression. You've been going around talking in this crazy Irish accent and acting so violently. It's like you became this person. I know it sounds stupid, but you weren't *you* anymore – you were *him*. That's what happened and that's why you don't remember these past five days."

Tim is incredulous. "So this Tumblety person really existed? You're telling me this was someone I used to be in a previous life?"

"Yes. That's exactly what I'm saying."

"I don't remember. I don't remember! What did I do?"

"Oh, Tim he was very, very bad man. Evil. He...you... murdered three women."

"Oh, God. No! Oh, God! How could I do that? What's going to happen to me? You've got to get me out of this nightmare. Please!"

Lucy and the two detectives watched Tim and Mary Jane from behind the two-way mirror. They could overhear every word of the conversation. Dubcek remained cynical. "So as soon as we bring him into custody, he snaps back to being sweet old Timothy Jeffries who never hurt a soul."

"I know I said Tumblety was a master con man but it's possible he might've snapped back to consciousness. I just don't know how or why that would suddenly happen."

"He wasn't exactly unconscious when he went on his killing spree, Ms. Carvallo," Jacobsen reminded her.

"Yes, he was, detective. That's exactly what he was."

"He's agreed to take a polygraph. See if he can fool that as easily as he's kidding his wife." Lucy gave Dubcek a look that suggested in no uncertain terms that she really didn't like him.

"How long have you known the Jeffries, Lucy?" asked Jacobsen, in a softer tone.

"I met MJ right after she married Tim. We worked out at the same health club. I met Tim several times but I never knew him that well. He was never the most sociable guy."

"Is it a good marriage?"

Lucy hesitated. "Well, you know. All marriages have their ups and downs."

"But was it more down than up?"

"Y'know, detective I really wasn't intimately acquainted with their relationship. Maybe you should ask MJ about it."

Defense attorney, Sheridan Parkes sat back in her studded brown leather chair behind a rich, mahogany desk. Two huge windows filled the large room with a dramatic, golden light. At fifty-two, she was an experienced and wily trial lawyer. Her dark arched eyebrows and strong jawline gave her a somewhat intimidating appearance with a demeanor to match. She was one smart cookie, as most prosecuting attorneys could attest. Mary Jane and Lucy listened to the sage professional. "Well, I've heard some wild stories in my years as a defense attorney but this one is truly remarkable."

"Sounds like you don't believe us, counselor?" Mary Jane said, sensing doubt in Ms. Parkes' tone.

"It's irrelevant whether I believe you, Mrs. Jeffries. It's what I can make a jury believe. If I'm fighting in your corner, I have to sell them an argument they can buy into. But let me cut to the chase -- this is never going to trial. Hate to be blunt but your husband is mentally incompetent."

"He's not insane, counselor," Mary Jane explained, realizing the attorney really didn't seem to grasp exactly what had happened to her husband. "Tim was not himself. He was Francis Tumblety.'

Lucy jumped in. "I channeled this person from 1888. It was like Tim Jeffries was asleep inside his own body."

"Hmmm…that's a really hard sell, guys. Juries might be unpredictable but there's no way they'll ever buy that. It sounds like a feeble excuse. Whoever your husband was in his mind is one thing but physically….he was the person who committed these crimes. His hands strangled then mutilated those three women."

"Yes but..." started Mary Jane but her attempted rebuttal was speedily over-ruled.

"The state's evidence against your husband is overwhelming yet he's totally convinced he's innocent of all charges. He passed the polygraph with flying colors which, in itself, is validation that your husband is psychologically deranged..." Mary Jane cut off the attorney.

"Well, I know for a fact he isn't psychologically deranged."

"Don't get upset with me, Mrs. Jeffries. I'm just laying out the facts for you. It actually works in your husband's favor. We don't want this case going before a jury. They'll convict him in a heartbeat. We need a judge who thinks he's not competent to stand trial."

"What are his chances, Ms. Parkes -- of being found innocent of these crimes?"

"Zero to none. He'll be institutionalized for the rest of his life."

"It's not right! I don't want him to be stuck in a mental home when he's perfectly sane. I want my husband back!"

"I'm sorry but getting your husband back is not an option, Mrs. Jeffries. Insanity is his only defense."

"And if he loses that option?"

"If he's found to be of sound mind and mentally fit to stand trial? The only good news is that here in the state of Illinois there's no longer a death penalty. He'll be locked up for the rest of his life with no chance of parole. And, as he'll have a degree of notoriety about him, he'll be a target, he'll probably spend most of his time in solitary for his own protection."

"Protection?"

"Cons like to score points! Imagine how much respect an inmate would gain amongst his peers if he slashed the throat of Jack the Ripper. That'd be quite a notch on his prison bedpost." The realization that her husband was going to be incarcerated for the rest of his natural life suddenly dawned on Mary Jane. Her focus had been on herself and the dreaded, fateful date of October 9th. With Tim behind bars, that was no longer a concern. The guilt of her affair with Derek was also playing on her mind. Sure, Tim had had his issues but she hadn't exactly been the most supportive wife. *He hadn't murdered these poor women, it was Francis Tumblety.* Tim was innocent but the law would never see it that way. It was now time for her to do whatever she could to save the man she was once very much in love with.

CHAPTER EIGHT

Tim looked a forlorn figure, wearing an orange inmate uniform as he stood before the judge at his arraignment hearing that afternoon. A smartly dressed Counselor Parkes stood with him while a prosecuting attorney looked on. The bespectacled judge read a document he was holding, then peered over his paper at Tim. "You are accused of three counts of murder in the first degree. Due to the severity of these charges, I will not be setting bail. Do you want to enter a plea?"

"Not guilty!" Tim yelled. The judge appeared quite disinterested in Tim's outburst of innocence.

"Trial date is set for December 17th." The judge banged his gavel to signify that he was done. Tim looked at Counselor Parkes with a totally confused expression as a police officer approached him.

"What happens now, counselor?"

"You'll be detained until your trial date."

"That's two months from now. Where will they put me?"

"You'll be given state protection." The officer took Tim by the arm and led him away as Counselor Parkes shuffled an assortment of legal papers and placed them in her briefcase.

"What does that mean?!" Tim yelled to her as he was taken out of the courtroom.

Tim's ankle was shackled to a bench seat in the back of a heavy duty police transport wagon as it headed for the Chicago State Penitentiary. The wagon drove up the long, lonely road that led to the large, imposing brownstone fortress with its high walls topped with rows of circled razor wire. The heavy iron gates opened as the wagon drove into a gravel forecourt. The wagon doors opened and Tim stumbled out, his ankles and hands shackled as two prison guards escorted him into the building for processing. He shuffled across the gravel forecourt and into the ominous building. "Inmate Jeffries, Timothy. 603562," called a voice, announcing the latest guest to check-in. His shackles were removed by two guards before being led along a corridor of depressingly dismal prison cells. All of them dirty white and empty. Tim was the day's only arrival. Halfway along they stopped at one particular empty cell. A guard pulled open the heavy white door with its small glass window of reinforced glass.

"Stand still," came the order. A prison guard unlocked his cuffs and freed his chafed wrists. "Make yourself comfortable," he grunted. Tim was pushed him into the small, stark and brightly lit room and the cell door slammed shut behind him. The only furniture in the cell, if you could call it that, was a steel bench bolted to the wall and a steel toilet with no seat. *How long would he be kept here? What was going to happen to him next?* All traces of the dynamic persona of Francis Tumblety were gone and Tim's new nightmare was about to begin. He sat on the cold bench and looked around at the small space that confined him. How in God's name had he ended up in such a desperate place? The events of the last twenty-four hours ran through his mind. *Why couldn't he remember anything since the party?* He stood up started to pace the cell, back and forth, back and forth, wracking his brains to try and trigger a memory that would help him make sense of all this. Those last five days were missing from his brain and as hard as he tried he couldn't unlock whatever had happened. In his mind, he was being charged with crimes he didn't do. He had so many questions but absolutely no answers.

It was a good hour before two prison guards returned and unlocked the cell door. These men were large, hulking figures who no sane person would mess with. "Stand up!" ordered one of them. Tim obeyed and stood passively. "Turn around!" Tim did as he was told. "Put your hands behind your back." Tim was silently compliant and the officer cuffed his wrists.

"Where are you taking me?" Neither guard answered. They walked Tim out and along the bleak row of empty cells. He was led through a heavy steel door, down a corridor, into an elevator and down a floor, through another steel door and into another prison block where the corridors seemed wider. Tim felt he was walking with two Neanderthals in uniforms A prisoner in a wheelchair rolled slowly towards him and the two guards. They exchanged glances but no words were spoken.

"Stop here," said one of the guards outside a room where a heavy set nurse was changing the paper sheet on a raise examination table. A balding man with overly thick library glasses and wearing a doctor's white coat entered from a side door.

"Sit over there," mumbled the doctor. Tim was very anxious, his mind still in turmoil. *What was happening?* He did as he was told and sat down on a small reclining table with his hands still cuffed behind his back. The doctor studied a sheet then looked up before ordering one of the guards to remove Tim's cuffs. "Remove your clothing." Tim slipped off his shoes then stood up, unbuttoned his orange prison uniform and stood naked in the middle of the room. "You can sit up here now." The doctor, tapped the top of the examination table as if ordering a puppy dog. Tim sat on the table feeling extremely vulnerable as anyone naked in front of strangers would, particularly in an environment that must have seen more than its fair share of extreme violence.

The doctor shone a flashlight into Tim's eyes. "Stick out your tongue." The doctor stuck a spatula into Tim's mouth. "Stand on the scale." Tim stood up and stepped on it. The nurse looked at the digital read out.

"One hundred and eighty seven."

"Against the wall, over there." Tim stood against various height lines etched on the white wall. The nurse read out the measurement.

"Five feet ten inches."

The doctor scribbled some notes then put down his pen and pulled on a pair of latex gloves. "Turn around and bend over," he said to Tim, as he squirted lubricant from a dispenser onto the fingers of his right hand.

"What for?"

"You heard the doc," snapped a prison guard.

"Cavity search is mandatory for new inmates," said the doctor without the slightest hint of any emotion. Tim reluctantly complied. The doctor lubed Tim's anus and inserted a finger. As well as feeling extremely uncomfortable, Tim was embarrassed to be so publicly humiliated in front of two guards and a female nurse. "Clear," the doctor announced. The nurse handed Tim a tissue to wipe himself dry. "You can put your underwear back on now," said the doctor, pulling off the latex gloves and dumping them in a trash can. He washed his hands while the nurse placed a thermometer under Tim's tongue. As Tim sat back down, she wrapped a rubber strip around his bicep and tightened. A thick vein in his arm started to bulge at the joint inside his elbow. She tapped it with her thumb then prepared a syringe. Tim watched as the needle entered his flesh, directly into the vein at the joint of his elbow. The nurse extracted enough blood to fill two vials. He looked away, clearly uncomfortable with the painful prick or the sight, which was duly noted by the two smirking guards.

"Guess you don't like the sight of blood when it's yours, huh?" Tim glanced at the uniformed caveman, then at his brutish colleague. These were two of the men who would be his keepers now until his trial date. Maybe they'd become his keepers for the rest of his living days.

It was lunchtime in the prison canteen. Tim stood in line with the other inmates as mashed potatoes, green beans and what looked like chicken were ladled onto plastic dinner trays. Each inmate took their food and plastic utensils and sat at a table of their choosing. Tim stared down at his food, not wanting to make eye contact with anyone. This was a dangerous environment, even more so for someone who had no idea of new inmate protocol. But he'd seen enough movies to get a solid clue that this was not a good time for socializing.

He took his tray and left the line. His eyes darted furtively around the large canteen for a space to sit down. He noticed a table near no one in particular and moved towards it. It felt as if everyone's eyes were trained on him. He sat silently, and stared at his plate of food, then stuck his white plastic fork into his mashed potato. It didn't look particularly appetizing and he was so uptight he couldn't even think about eating anything.

Amongst the sixty or so inmate diners, there was little conversation. Along the four walls stood armed prison guards. If anyone was motivated enough to start any trouble, they would be the ones finishing it. It seemed most of the prisoners sat in their own ethnic groups; blacks, Latinos, white skinheads while the rest of misfit inmates were a collection of elderly, crazy or just plain scary.

A rogue skinhead saw Tim sitting by himself and decided to join him. Tim glanced up at the twenty-something inmate as he sat down opposite him. His neck was heavily tattooed, very poorly, in black ink and his wide-eyed excited smile did nothing to calm Tim's edginess. "You the guy who killed the three bitches?" Tim remained silent. He stared down at his plate and kept eating. His enthusiastic dining companion wanted an answer. "You that guy, right?" Tim said nothing. "Huh? Huh?" Tim looked up slowly.

"So they tell me," Tim mumbled. The young skinhead laughed.

"Oh, you an evil cunt. I'm staying clear of you, evil cunt. Watch your back. Better watch your back. This is an evil place. You gonna fit right in, evil cunt." Tim continued to eat, pretending not to listen. The young skinhead wanted more reaction from this new and already notorious inmate but it wasn't forthcoming. His fixed stare was fixed on Tim and now he was agitated. He stabbed into his chicken and chewed up a large mouthful. *Bammm!* He slammed down his fist on the table. Tim quickly looked up. *Splaaat!* The skinhead spat a big mouthful of chewed food in Tim's face then laughed hysterically. Inwardly, Tim was freaked out but tried to stay calm as he wiped the gobs of slushy, masticated food off of his face. "Weeeeeeeeee!" squealed Tim's manic provocateur.

In her trendy downtown loft, Lucy opened the front door to Harold Meeks, the retired elderly neighbor from the party, beaming a smile at her. "Hello, sweetheart. How you are doing? That really was a wonderful party the other night."

"Thank you. Come on in, Harold. Thanks for coming over."

"Well, it wasn't like I had too far to travel!" Harold joked as he followed Lucy into the living room where Mary Jane was sitting. His eyes lit up again. "I remember you from Lucy's party!"

"Oh, good, you remember MJ. Her husband was Tim."

"Hello, Harold. Nice to see you again," smiled Mary Jane. Harold sat down opposite her on the large, fluffy white sofa and made himself comfortable. "Yes, I remember you and your husband. Lost his job he was telling me. Poor fella. Nice guy, too."

"Can I get you anything, Harold? I can open some wine."

"No thanks, Lucy. I'm just so curious to know why you wanted me to visit. You mentioned something about my old job."

Lucy smiled. "Well, yes. We need some help rather urgently and I immediately thought of you."

"My pleasure. Anything to break up the boredom of retirement. What do you need? Whatever it is, I'm in!" Lucy sat down beside Mary Jane. Both their demeanors turned serious. "Uh-oh, this isn't good, is it?"

"Well, put it this way, MJ's husband isn't doing too well. He's got himself into a tricky situation and we think you're the perfect person to help us, seeing as you know about the prison system and its inner workings."

"Say no more. I'm your man! Your Tim's gone and got himself some trouble, hasn't he? I knew it. He was way too drunk to drive home after the party. Those cops stopped him didn't they? The sons of bitches."

"Well, that's close enough," said Mary Jane, looking at Lucy. Harold wasn't finished. "Got himself a couple of days in the Graybar Hotel, has he?"

"Yup, you guessed that right, Harold," smiled Lucy.

"I can get him some nice filet mignon smuggled into him. Not a problem. Is that it?" Harold smiled at his own misguided intuition and waited for the two women to acknowledge it. Lucy sighed.

"No, Harold. That's not it," said Lucy, getting serious. "We want to get him out of there." Harold stared at the two women with an expression of sheer delight.

"A jail break? Holy cow! You two women are as crazy as I am. Wow!" The two women didn't know couldn't tell if Harold was for it, or against it. Harold sat back in his chair and rolled his eyes to the ceiling. "Wow, wow, wow!" He rocked forward and stared silently at the shag carpet. "Okay, we need a really smart plan if we're going to pull this off and I know exactly how we do it."

Lucy winked at Mary Jane.

In the bright, white confines of the prison visitors area of Chicago State Penitentiary, Mary Jane sat behind a bulletproof glass partition and looked at her sorry-looking husband. They both held telephones to communicate. Tim was scared and Mary Jane could see it in is eyes. "This place is killing me. It's full of fucking murderers." Tim didn't seem to grasp that that was precisely why he was there. Mary Jane commiserated. "It's going to be okay, Tim. Lower your voice."

"How? How is this ever going to be okay? I'll be lucky to make it out alive to my trial date."

"We're going to help you."

"We? Who's we? I don't think Counselor Parkes has done me any favors. She couldn't even get bail for me."

"No, not her."

"Who then? You can't help me. I'm alone in here."

"Do you remember Harold Meeks from Lucy's party?"

"No. I don't remember Harold Meeks. Why should I?"

"He was the elderly gentleman you were talking to for a while." Tim's brow furrowed as he tried to remember the details of that fateful night.

"Yeah, yeah, I remember talking to some old guy now you mention it. So what?"

"He's going to be paying you a visit."

"What good is that going to do me?"

"It will, Tim. Believe me, it will."

The following morning, a Fresfro food service delivery van pulled up outside the rear gates of the state penitentiary. Harold Meeks was behind the wheel with Lucy Carvallo beside him - both wearing Fresfro food company uniforms. "Okay, here we go, Lucy. As I told you, they'll be two guards. One outside with the Matron. That'll be Slick Micky. He knows me. When we get inside, we'll run into Boomer who's a nosey sonofabitch. I'll keep Boomer talking while you make the delivery. You keep walking. Take the stairs up to the second floor. If you run into any guards, tell them you need a signature from Dave Riggins."

"Who's he?"

"Doesn't matter. That'll make you sound kosher. In five minutes, they'll be starting the first lunch session. What does Tim know?"

"Nothing at all. MJ was nervous they listen in on the phones."

"Good. They do. Less he knows the better at this point."

"I'm really nervous about this, Harold. I hope I'll be okay. Thanks for doing this."

"You kidding me? I'd do anything for you, sweetheart. You know that. Anyway, sure beats sitting on my ass watching golf on the TV. You got the bag?" Harold asked, wondering where it was. Lucy tapped her breasts, which appeared larger than usual under her Fresfro uniform.

"Stuck it in here. How d'you like my new double D's?"

"Clever girl. Those guards are going to love you! Okay, let's go." Harold and Lucy got out of the delivery van and unloaded several food trays, carry them into the austere building. Slick Micky greeted them.

"Mr. Meeks! Thought you retired last year!"

"Hi, Micky. Yeah, they needed some extra help so they called the old geezer back. After thirty years in the business, a few extra days couldn't hurt."

"Boomer'll wanna bend your ear as usual."

"Same old Boomer, huh?" chuckled Harold as he carried the tray past Slick Micky who ogled Lucy. "Who's this, your grandkid?" chuckled the rough looking guard. Lucy smiled at him as she walked past with the food tray but she didn't want to talk. "Damn, she's cute."

"She's new, so be nice," Harold warned teasingly as Micky grabbed the handle on one of the heavy metal back doors and yanked it open for them. Harold led Lucy through into the delivery station where an enormous hulking figure was sitting, staring at a computer screen. "Hi, Boomer," said Harold, nonchalantly. "I'm back!" Boomer looked up from the screen and sat back in his chair. "And you're bigger than ever!"

"Well, well, the old man returns! Thought you were sent out to pasture." Harold and Lucy dumped down the trays they were carrying. Lucy went straight back outside to bring in another one while Harold deliberately started up a conversation with the enormous prison guard. "Got yourself a pretty co-worker this time, too, huh?"

"Sure. Why not?" Harold joked. "Hey, Boomer – you gotta

stop eating all the food us guys bring in here.

"You kidding? I lost five pounds last week."

"Yeah? You should try losing a hundred and five pounds, you fat bastard."

"So what happened? Fresfro couldn't function without you? They dragged you out of retirement?"

"Something like that." Harold lied. Lucy brought in a second tray and dumped it down on top of the others. "Hey, Boomer. I gotta show you something." Harold turned his back on Lucy and nodded for Boomer to do the same. He took out a copy of Juggs magazine from inside his overalls. "Check this out."

"What you got there, you dirty old man?"

"I know how much you like those big titty babes and you gotta see this one. She's a knockout – nipples you could hang your coat on." As the two men started flipping through the pages of the colorful girly mag, Lucy made her way up the stairs to the first level, holding bogus paperwork in her hand. She walked slowly to not look suspicious. At the top of the first flight, a heavy bar-stop door greeted her. She shoved against it but it seemed to be locked. "Shit!" she screamed inwardly. Now Lucy was really anxious. She looked through the wired glass that gave her a narrow view of a hallway. She could see a prison guard was seated close by so she banged on the glass to get his attention. The guard stood up and approached the other side of the door. Lucy pointed to the logo on her Fresfro hat and he nodded then punched in a code on a keypad lock and the door opened.

"This is a restricted area. Who let you up here?"

"Boomer said it was okay. I need Dave Riggins to sign this," said Lucy, holding up the paperwork.

"Boomer knows better than that. Dave ain't here. He's in the cafeteria and that's a priority restricted area so you sure ain't going back there."

"Okay, I'll tell Boomer we'll just have to take today's delivery back."

The guard looked at his watch. "It's lunchtime for the inmates. He won't leave the cafeteria for another hour. Give it here. I'll take it to him." He reached out to take the document. Lucy was reluctant to give it up. Harold hadn't mentioned a third guard. "You want it signed or not?"

Lucy knew she had to give him the paperwork or it would appear too suspicious. "Sure, that's fine. Didn't want to put you out, that's all," Lucy lied, handing over the documents. The guard smirked.

"I got nothing else to do. All the inmates are eating so I'm just guarding empty cells." Seeing Lucy was a welcome sight for a man who spent every working day in a building full of angry testosterone.

"Thanks," she smiled, flirtatiously.

"Wait there. Don't move! You'll get me into trouble."

"Sure."

Lucy watched the guard walk away down the corridor carrying

the paperwork. She would only have a few minutes. Looking down the row of cells, she hurried along the corridor. She looked into each cell, one by one, looking for the marker Mary Jane had told Tim to leave – a white sock in the middle of the cell floor. It was the only way Lucy would know for sure which cell Tim had been put in. Each small cell had a bed and a toilet with little else. There was nothing to tell them apart.

Bingo! There was the sock, right where she was expecting to see one. Lucy unbuttoned her overall and pulled out a small, white laundry bag. She tossed it into the cell then buttoned up her uniform and hurried back to where the guard had told her to wait. She stood by the door and took a deep breath to try and slow her racing heartbeat. The guard hadn't returned. *Maybe he'd twigged that she was an imposter.* She grabbed the door and twisted the handle. It was locked. She used both hands to try and twist it. The door weighed a ton and there was no way it was going to open without the code. She was panicked when she heard the guards footsteps getting louder and closer. She quickly let go of the handle and tried to compose herself. "Guess I was wrong. It's his day off today. Get Boomer to sign it, that'll be fine," said the guard, handing the paperwork back.

"Sorry. I'm new. I didn't know that." The guard keyed in the code, allowing Lucy to go back downstairs where Boomer and Harold were staring at a centerfold of a naked model. "Can we go now, Mr. Meeks?" called out Lucy, acting impatiently. Harold averted his gaze from the magazine and shoved it over to Boomer.

"Keep it," he said to the large prison guard. Harold winked at Lucy and the two of them walked out of the delivery station and heading back to the Fresfro van. "See you tomorrow, Boomer!" shouted Harold.

"Sure! Thanks, old man!"

Mary Jane packed her suitcase at Lucy's condo, ready to head back to Delmar Avenue. She was heading home again and no longer in fear for her life. She walked into the kitchen where Lucy was pouring three glasses of Pinot Grigio. "I think we all need this after today's little adventure. I still can't believe we managed to pull it off. I mean -- it all went according to plan, just as you wanted, MJ. Thanks to Harold's insider knowledge and brilliant planning."

"He's a gem. Well, I guess it's up to Tim now." The toilet flushed and Harold Meeks came out of the bathroom zipping up his fly.

"Phew....my prostate isn't what it used to be. I can't hold it in for more than thirty minutes. I tell ya, ladies -- growing old sucks." Lucy handed him a glass of vino.

"Well, I guess you'll just have to refill that leaky bladder."

"Thanks, sweetheart. Boy, that was a fun day out today. Just what I needed. They totally bought it!" They clinked their wine glasses and raised them in the air with a collective celebratory *Cheers!*

"Let's see if it goes as smoothly tomorrow," warned Lucy. "I don't think we broke the law today but we were close."

Harold hoisted himself up on a barstool at the kitchen counter and plonked himself down. "All we did was make a delivery. Nothing unlawful about feeding the hungry."

Mary Jane gulped a mouthful of Pinot and huffed out a sigh. "I've been a shitty wife. I haven't been there for Tim these last couple of years. He's needed me and I've just given him shit. And that affair with Derek was just dumb." Lucy and Harold said nothing. They knew what Mary Jane was planning was wrong but they had no intention of backing out now. "I've gotta do this for him. I just don't see any other option. I mean, they'll never let him out, will they?"

Lucy look concerned for her friend. "Well, Derek's over now so that's all behind you. Don't be so hard on yourself, MJ. You and Tim had issues, that's true. When money's tight, it causes all sorts of stress."

"Well, it's too late to stop our devious little plan now, ladies," said Harold, sounding like a stern army captain about to lead his soldiers into enemy territory. "The wheels are fully in motion and I'm driving." Harold's devil-may-care attitude had given both women Dutch courage to carry out their extremely risky escapade. They were in danger of becoming criminals themselves and everyone knew it.

"Thanks for putting your butts on the line, guys. That was brave going in there today."

"Walk in the park. I've done it thousands of times," chuckled Harold though Lucy was still guilt-ridden; not for the prison visit, for getting the Jeffries in this terrible situation.

"Jesus, it was the least I could do, MJ -- seeing as I was the root cause of this fucking nightmare." The three of them fell silent. Harold looked concerned at the two women. He knew they were now in deep and it showed on both their worried faces. He tried to offer up some hope.

"Look Mary Jane. I don't know you as well as Lucy here does but have you really thought this all the way through?" Mary Jane downed the rest of her wine and refilled her glass with chilled bottle of Pinot.

"Yes, I have. I know what I'm doing, Harold. I've got a plan and the less you both know about it the better. You can't tell the authorities what you don't know."

CHAPTER NINE

It was early morning but Tim wouldn't have known it as he sat on his bed staring up at ceiling in his cell. Accused of a triple homicide, his life in the general prison populous was perilous. He'd rather be locked up in solitary than have to deal with the madness of the other inmates but that was now a moot point. The laundry bag Lucy had dropped yesterday was to be his savior. Everything he needed was in there, including detailed instructions, but he wouldn't need any of the contents until the lunch break. It was now about timing if this was to work. He ran the impending scenario through his head, over and over. This had to be done right but things go wrong as things do, and you can't plan for that. But in the prison environment, even Tim was aware that consistent structure was the key to control, which is why everything worked like clockwork. That would be an advantage. After an uneventful breakfast shoved through the small opening in his cell door at 7 a.m., Tim waited for the hours to pass.

The lunch bell range dead on the noon hour. Each inmate stood by the door waiting for the electronic doors to open simultaneously. Each prisoner stood in their respective doorways to be counted before walking single-file down the corridor to the cafeteria. All present and correct, the guard on duty blew his whistle and the inmates started walking -- all except Tim. He ducked back into his cell and rifled through the laundry bag. As quickly as he could, he stripped off and pulled a Fresfro uniform from the laundry bag. He buttoned up the overall, pulled the baseball style hat firmly over his head, then put on the false brown moustache and spectacles. At the bottom of the bag was some bogus paperwork just like Lucy had. He stood inside his cell and stared at the door Lucy had used the day before. Where was she?

Harold drove the Fresfro van drove in to the delivery bay of The Metropolitan Correctional Center, same as the previous day with Lucy beside him. "Remember, that door you couldn't open at the top of the stairs is only locked on the inmate side. It's not locked on your side."

"It was locked yesterday," Lucy assured him. Harold shook his head.

"No, it wasn't. The guards use it all the time if there's trouble on that floor – in case they need to access that level quickly but it's a seriously heavy door. You really have to shove it hard to open it from the stairwell. But if it closes behind you, the only way to get back down those stairs is to punch in the code. That'll automatically open it."

"Tell me about it. What's the code?"

"Hell if I know. I was only ever the food delivery guy. Even if I knew the code for yesterday it wouldn't work today because every day they change it. That guard on duty is the only person who knows those numbers."

"So if I get stuck up there…"

"It's over, sweetheart. As cute as you are, you won't be able to flirt your way out of there with any of those guys. They're all hard headed screws at the end of the day."

They parked and got out. Lucy swung open the back doors and pulled out a food tray just like the day before. She carried it into the prison building while Harold walked over to chat with Slick Micky. "Brought your grandkid along again, I see."

"Why not? Her legs have more energy in them than mine."

"Bet they're a damn sight prettier than yours, too."

"That's not fair, Micky. You've never seen my beautiful legs," joked Harold. He rolled up his pants leg. "Look at that!" Micky wasn't impressed.

"Damn. That's an ugly old leg." Lucy walked in carrying her large food tray past Boomer and placed her food tray on a long table in the delivery area.

"Hi, Boomer!" Boomer looked up and gave her a dirty smile.

"Where's grandpa today?"

"He's blabbing with Micky."

"Figured."

Lucy turned to leave to get another food tray. "Oh, Harold said he lent you something yesterday. Said he needs it back. I can take it if you want." Boomer looked suddenly embarrassed.

"No, no. I'll take it out to him." The large guard shuffled the papers on his table and opened a drawer. Lucy pretended not to notice as he rolled up the girly magazine, got up and waddled outside with it. Lucy took that as her cue to head up the stairs. Looking through the small wired glass window, she watched the same guard from yesterday walk behind the last of the inmates towards the cafeteria. The coast was clear. Tim had less than a minute now and the timing had to be perfect. He slipped out of his cell and walked quickly towards the key coded door that Lucy couldn't budge the day before.

Baammm! Lucy threw her entire body weight into the metal door and cracked it open just enough. Tim grabbed it and ducked into the stairwell, following her down the stairs. They both remained silent as Lucy led Tim down. As they got into the services area they were greeted by the imposing figure of Boomer standing in front of a nervous Harold. "What're you guys doing up there? That's a restricted area."

"Billy's new," smiled Lucy. "I'm training him. He didn't know that area's off limits."

Boomer eyed them suspiciously. "You're the new gal training the new guy? That's kinda dumb. Hey, Harold why they bring you back when you got a new guy?"

"Ohhhh…." Harold winced, clutching his chest. "Uhhh…!" He winced again and staggered over to the wall, slumping down in a heap.

"Oh, shit!" cried Lucy, running over to Harold and leaving Tim looking helpless. "I think he's having a heart attack! Billy! Get Mr. Meeks' pills from the van!" Tim ran outside as Boomer knelt down besides the rapidly deteriorating Harold and shouted into his walkie-talkie. "Micky, get in here."

"He should never have come back to work at his age," said Lucy, loosening Harold's tie and unbuttoning his collar as he gasped for air.

"Uhhhhhh," he stuttered, wincing in agonizing pain. Micky came running in and knelt down beside Lucy and Boomer as they supported Harold, still lying on the ground.

"What the crap? Guy outside said he suffered a heart attack."

"What the crap happened here?" said Micky.

"We have to get him to a hospital."

"I'll get an ambulance," said Boomer, concerned about his old friend who seemed to be fading fast. "Where's that guy with his pills?" he asked, looking around.

"No time! Billy can drive him there before any ambulance gets here. Can you two help me carry him out to the van?" Boomer leant over like a gentle giant and carefully picked up Harold's limp body. Micky ran to hold open the outside door as Boomer walked out with him in his arms towards the van. Tim was sitting in the driver's seat, rummaging through the glove box. Lucy ran over to him. "Where are his pills, Billy?" Lucy yelled.

"I can't find them!" Tim yelled back.

Micky opened the back door of the van as Boomer lowered Harold in, placing him down carefully. Lucy jumped in the passenger side, opened the glove compartment and took out a plastic container full of blue pills. She showed them to Tim. "What's this then? Jesus, Billy! Let's move!" She clambered into the back of the van to sit with Harold as Boomer gently closed the back off the van. "Thanks, guys!" she called out to Boomer and Micky as the two guards watched the Fresfro van speed out of the iron gates onto the side street. "Everyone okay?" Lucy asked, as Harold sat up and smiled.

"Phew! We did it!"

"They won't know I'm missing until after lunch. What's the plan now?" Tim asked.

"We're heading back to your house where your wife is waiting to drive you somewhere a million miles from here, I guess."

"You don't know?" Tim asked anxiously. Harold sat up.

"She wouldn't tell us."

"How are you two gonna explain breaking me out of there?"

"Don't worry about us, Tim. You just make sure you and Mary Jane get as far away from here as you can. You're on borrowed time," said Harold, not that Tim didn't know it already. They headed towards Delmar Avenue not knowing how this was all going to play out but Lucy had done her part. At the very least, Tim was back to his old self but how long he could remain a free man was anyone's guess. It wouldn't be long before the alarm would be raised and the police would be scouring the entire city of Chicago. One of the first places they'd head to would be Delmar Avenue so every second counted now. The Fresfro van pulled up outside the Jeffries' house. Lucy gave Tim an encouraging smile, not knowing if she'd ever see him again. "Goodbye, Tim. Sorry it's ending like this."

Harold leaned over from the rear of the van and shook Tim's hand. "All the best, my friend."

"Thanks guys." Tim jumped out and ran to the house. Mary Jane watched from the living room window as Lucy and Harold drove away. Mary Jane ushered Tim inside, closing the door quickly behind him and hugging him tight. It was the first time they'd embraced in years and it felt good – really good. Tim broke away from her embrace and started getting out of his overalls. "What's the plan?" he asked, anxiously.

"Everything is set, Tim. Get changed and we'll go."

"Go where?" Mary Jane led Tim into the living room where she had a fresh hospital gown waiting for him.

"Put that on."

"Why?"

"I'm taking you to the hospital."

Tim looked at her. "Are you serious?"

"I'm checking you in as a patient and keeping you in a private room -- for months if I have to." It was a strange way to hide him, Tim thought. It would certainly buy him time though. With Mary Jane's senior position as a manager at the hospital, he could stay hidden there and under the radar. "I've already prepared all the documentation for your admission. We'll wait till everything quiets down and then I'll move you out to wherever we decide to spend the rest of our lives together. I'm so sorry for my terrible behavior, for everything bad I did, Tim."

Tim kissed his wife. "Just don't let them take me back to that hell hole of a place. That's all I ask."

"Don't worry, honey. I'll protect you and keep you safe. You won't need clothes. Nothing here needs to change. Even your toiletries need to stay just as they are so the police won't think you ever came here. But you'll need to change your appearance in case anyone at the hospital recognizes you."

"I'll shave my head and eyebrows," said Tim, as he headed to the bathroom.

"Okay but do it fast! Then put on this hospital gown," Mary Jane called out. She looked through the window to see if there was any unusual activity outside. Everything appeared normal. She could hear Tim running the faucets in the bathroom. "Hurry, Tim! Every minute counts!" She was getting extremely jumpy. She anxiously paced the floor. The minutes passed. Tim seemed to be taking forever. The water in the sink was still running. She hurried to the bathroom and tapped on the door. "Tim! You'd better get a move on in there!" Tim didn't answer. All she could hear was the water running. She twisted the handle to open the door but it was locked. "Tim! We really need to get going!"

Brrrnnnggg!

"Shit!" Mary Jane whispered to herself. "Tim! There's someone at the door." Tim didn't answer. Mary Jane froze. She didn't know what to do.

Brrrnnnggg!

She hurried to the window to see if she could see who was standing on her doorstep, ringing the doorbell. It was Derek. That was the last person she needed to see right now. Derek glanced at the window and saw Mary Jane duck away from view.

Brrrnnnggg! Brrrnnnggg!

Mary Jane's mind was racing now. How could she get Tim out of the house without Derek seeing them? She hurried back to the bathroom just as Tim opened the door and emerged with his head and eyebrows shaved to the skin. It was a startling transformation. "Ohh! You look so different." Tim said nothing. "Change of plan. We have to leave out the back. We'll grab a taxi on Sweetbriar." Tim stood motionless in the bathroom doorway looking at Mary Jane with an icy look in his cold, pale blue eyes. "You feeling okay, honey?"

"I'll leave when I'm ready to leave," said Tim, in a strong Irish brogue. "And I'm not your honey." Mary Jane stood rigid with fear.

"Tim, don't talk like that. It's not funny." She stepped back slowly into the hallway. Tim had to be messing with her.

Brrrnnnggg! Brrrnnnggg!

"No woman tells me what to do!" shouted Tim, as he headed to the front door. Mary Jane ran upstairs in a blind panic.

Brrrnnnggg! Brrrnnnggg!

Tim yanked open the front door to see Derek standing in front of him.

"Holy shit! Who are you?" asked Derek, not recognizing Tim and certainly not expecting to see the unsettling sight of a man with a shaved head and eyebrows.

"I might ask you the same question!" Tim grabbed Derek by the collar and dragged him inside, kicking the door shut behind him. He threw Derek back against the door, grabbed him again and head-butted him in the face.

"Uuuhhhh…!" Derek groaned, as he slumped down to the ground in a heap, his nose was split into a bloody mess. Tim turned around and looked up the stairs for Mary Jane. Now it was her turn.

"So you have gentleman caller's do you?" Tim yelled out in the distinct accent of Francis Tumblety as he walked menacingly up the staircase. "Is that how you earn your living, as a whore?!" Tim stood at the top of the stairs and stopped. He listened. He could hear Mary Jane rummaging around in the bedroom. "Let me show you how I deal with women of your persuasion!" He walked towards the bedroom and opened the door. Mary Jane was cowering in the corner, too terrified to move.

"You're still him, aren't you?"

"Dr. Tumblety at your service. But you can call me Jack." His mouth contorted into an evil smile. Mary Jane was shaking; trembling with fear.

"How? Why are you back?"

Tim frowned. "Back? I never left, you stupid woman."

"Where's Tim? What have you done to my husband?"

Tim smiled. "My name's Tim Jeffries," he said in her husband's normal mid-western accent. "I live at number forty-eight Delmar Avenue. I want to speak with my wife and I want to know why I'm dressed like this."

Mary Jane covered her mouth in disbelief. "It was you all along!" She looked over at the day calendar on her beside table and read the date: October 9th. "Oh, no. Please, God!"

Tim pulled out a cut-throat razor. The same one he'd just used to shave his head and eyebrows. Mary Jane started to move away from the wall. She pulled a gun from behind her back and pointed it at Tim.

"Get away from me, you fucking monster!"

Slaaaammmm! The bedroom door smashed open as Derek came bursting in. Tim spun around as Derek lunged at him with both hands. Tim waved his arm deftly, like an expert swordsman and sliced Derek's neck open with one horizontal slash. Derek staggered backwards, clutching his neck in a helpless attempt to stop the blood gushing out from his jugular vein. "Oooohhh!" gasped Mary Jane, now standing frozen and wide-eyed in disbelief as Derek collapsed to the ground, trying to gurgle out something. The gun shook in her two hands but her adrenalin rush was causing her to shake too much to squeeze the trigger. Tim turned back to Mary Jane, expressionless; a cold, dead look in his eyes.

"Blame my mother," he whispered in his Irish accent. "Back to business." He stood a less than six feet from Mary Jane, who still pointed the gun directly at his face.

"One more step and I'll shoot you back to 1888."

"You wouldn't shoot your own husband, would you?"

"No, I wouldn't. But you're not my husband." Tim swung his arm at the gun, knocking it out of her hands. It landed with a thump on the carpet.

Baaammm! Tim smashed his fist across her face. Mary Jane fell on the bed, groaning. Tim leapt on top of her, straddling her body and pinning her to the bed. His strong right hand gripped her throat like a metal vice clamping a piece of wood. The veins on his hand bulged with his powerful grasp as Mary Jane gasped for air. His expression became trance-like. Licking the blade of the razor to check its sharpness, he put it up against the soft flesh of her neck. "Holy Father Great God Lord Almighty I commit the soul of this angel of Beelzebub..."

"Noooooo...!" shouted Derek, lying on the floor behind him. He was barely alive but mustering his last breath he let out a yell. Tim was caught off guard. He leapt off Mary Jane to fend of any possible attack by Derek, giving Mary Jane enough time to quickly roll off the bed onto the floor clutching her neck and gasping for air. Tim grabbed Derek's head and smashed it against the floor, over and over and over again.

"Stop! Stop!" screamed Mary Jane, watching helplessly as Tim pummeled Derek's already broken body. "He can't hurt you anymore!" Derek lay motionless, a pool of blood under his skull. Tim turned his attention back to Mary Jane but now she was on the other side of the room with the gun back in her hands with it pointing at her would-be assassin. His expression softened as a soft smile crossed his face.

"Don't do anything you're going to regret, Mary Jane," said Tim, talking in his normal voice once again.

"Fuck you."

"Mary Jane, it's me. It's Tim. I love you, you know that. I would never hurt you."

"Goodbye – whoever you are." Mary Jane aimed the gun at his face and squeezed the trigger.

Click.

The chamber was empty. Mary Jane looked at the gun in disbelief. Tim stood in front of her, laughing. "Where's a bullet when you need one?" he said, returning to his Irish brogue again. "By this time tomorrow, I'll be back home in New York. But I'd like a little keepsake to remember you by. You never had any children, did you?

So why waste a perfectly good uterus in that useless body of yours?" Tim took a step towards her. Mary Jane desperately squeezed the trigger again.

BANG!!!! A bullet flew out the barrel and hit Tim between his steely eyes. The top of his head exploded like a watermelon, splattering the walls and Mary Jane with blood. Tim stared at her in disbelief.

BANG!!! Another bullet shot through his chest and into the wall behind him.

BANG!!! Another shot tore a hole in his abdomen. Tim's body fell back onto the bed, motionless and silent, his steel blue eyes staring coldly up at the ceiling.

Mary Jane dropped the gun. She sat up and looked across at the deadly carnage in her bedroom. Two dead men lay on the ground a few feet away. Their blood was splattered everywhere she looked. She'd once loved both of them but that seemed a million years ago now.

It was over.

THE END

EPILOGUE

Francis Tumblety evaded Scotland Yard detectives and
returned to America in 1888. Identical Ripper murders
of prostitutes continued in New York until 1903 –
the year Francis Tumblety died.

ABOUT THE AUTHOR

Tony Cane-Honeysett was born in in London, England. He attended Westminster City Grammar School and graduated from Ealing College of Art and Design. As well as being an author, Tony is also an Emmy Award winning filmmaker. His films include *The Royal Academy, Mondo Bondo* and *Mistreated*. In 2006, he was the recipient of the Individual Artist Fellowship for Media Studies awarded by The Tennessee Arts Commission. He has worked professionally as a copywriter for over 20 years in England and America, where he currently resides. He is also the author of *Fem Dom*.

www.ingramcontent.com/pod-product-compliance
Lightning Source LLC
Chambersburg PA
CBHW020124180626
46810CB00004B/1402